Avenged Revelator

A woman with something missing; her childhood was brutally stolen, her young life missed and only one thing on her mind, vengeance. Can she out ride the pain, can she avenge the past? Or is she doomed like her father before her?

Book 3 of the Revelator Trilogy

Mark Huck

Brew Town Media Publications

Copyright ©Mark Huck 2023

The author asserts the moral right to

Be identified as the author of this work

Published by Brew Town Media 2023

All rights reserved. No part of this publication may be reproduced, stored in a retrieval system, or transmitted in any form or by any means, electronic, mechanical, photocopying, recording or otherwise, without the prior permission of the author.

This book is sold subject to condition that it shall not, by way of trade or otherwise, be lent, resold, hired out or otherwise circulated without the author's prior consent in any form of binding or cover other than that in which it is published and without a similar condition including this condition being imposed on the subsequent purchaser.

Brew Town Media Publications

When you are lost, you need love, for when you are found you will need to give love.

Dedicated to those, that show you the way when you are lost.

The Roaming Revelator

CHAPTER 1: RIDE OF THE BANSHEE

The wail of an old carburettor-engine bike flooded the tranquil village as Dani raced through on her back wheel, playing with the bike as she dropped the front wheel back down again. The bike weaved through a crowded market place. She knocked over market stalls and screamed at anyone who tried to challenge her.

"Fuck you! You don't own me! Fuck you all!"

Tearing along the dusty dirt road, a crowd of angry people disappeared from the mirrors. She hated the world and everyone in it; no one had ever managed to tame her. Indy had tried to love her, tried to guide her. The only thing that ever worked was stories of her Dad.

Dani skidded the bike to a stop, throwing up a dusty dirt cloud just before she reached the gateway to top of the Harz Mountains. She stood where she had been told her mum and dad had nearly been killed by a wolf.

"Come on Mother Fucker! Vengeance will be mine!"

Many times she had stood on this empty road and bayed for the wolf to come, with one hand on her wooden-handled, full-tang hunting knife and one on the old pistol her granddad had left hidden in his toolbox, she stood motionless wanting to show her fight to anyone.

The only people she had ever respected were dead before she knew them. A few had come close. Indy had nearly tamed her, but the wild side of Dani had been too strong to break. From a young girl, she had heard many times, "What would Dan do?"

Slowly riding her bike into the American-style diner-come-garage that her granddad had built, she saw Indy, weak and pathetic. Dani loved her but could not express it. She had some respect for her for trying to do the right things, trying to bring her up, giving her morals and teaching her about her mum and dad, but she did not respect her fully. She saw a feeble woman who had been walked over by many people and failed to save her dad.

Indy wept as she knelt on the floor, picking up broken furniture parts and shards of glass. Her mum and dad had loved this place so much.

Dani growled her words - like her father had done when he knew he was in the wrong and unable to admit it.

"Leave it, Indy. Just fuckin' leave it."

Dani stood tall, just like her dad had always done; she towered above Indy, whose tears now dripped from her high cheek bones. She wept.

"Your dad loved it in these mountains. Why do you hate it so much?"

Danielle's face screwed up as she made a sucking noise through her teeth.

"Well, the world killed my parents and my granddad. The world fuckin' hates me. So, screw the world and everyone in it!"

Indy's tears became heavier. Dani's distaste for emotional people sent her into a rage. Dani screamed at Indy, with rage shooting from her fierce tongue. She forcefully told of how the world owed her for taking her family away. The world burned her before she could grow into it. Everywhere Dani was, pain and suffering was nigh. It followed her. She was dark of heart, dark of soul and dark of mind.

Whilst she still shouted her words, Indy rocked in the corner crying. Her blonde, matted hair stuck to her tears. Her thoughts spiralled with what Dan would do if he could see his daughter behaving like this. Dani stomped out of the room. Her words now calm but strong.

"I am taking my dad's bike. I may be some time."

She sat on the terror machine of death - the old street fighter that put her dad in prison for imposing retribution on her grandma's killer.

"I'll kill that bitch, Tania. And everyone else who's crossed us."

She started the raucous bike that she had restored with Otto. She had ensured every last detail was as her dad had intended. Even spraying it British racing green and learning to fade in a metallic black, just like it was when the bike of mayhem first rolled out with her dad aboard. It was a Genesis bike for her that she had personally collected from the police impound with Jack. The build list her dad had ticked off was still under the seat, slightly charred, but intact. It was the first bike her dad had built and the first that she had built. The restoration was a love affair with a time she had never been part of, putting the bike back to how her dad had it when he first passed his motorbike test. Making her feel happy and calm, like a child sat on a father's lap, a comforting feeling of nostalgia swamped her every time she saw it.

She was brave. She was dangerous. And she hated the police; she believed the police killed her dad.

In reality, only one person had killed him.

Indy had tried to show her that the whole police force was not like Tania, but she could not listen whilst her head and heart were full of rage.

She roared along the road, passing Otto's house, she left nothing but pain behind her. They had all tried to save her, even Jack. She wanted what she could not have, and that, was her mum and dad.

As the dust behind her settled, it fell gently from her aggressive exit past the houses. Wooden cabins that should have been so full of love yet were empty just like her heart, faded. She thought once again of the words she had heard Indy say under her breath nearly every day.

"What would Dan Do?"

She had heard many people say them over the years. Now was the time to do what her dad would have done!

The gravel under her tyres was like ice, sending both wheels sliding and both wheels spinning as she powered out of the bends. A misspent youth riding motorbikes across dirt roads and fields had taught her well. She had never found a person that could keep up with her when she raged. When her mind exploded and when her blood ran cold, it forced out the wild banshee she carried with her, wailing in pain and sorrow. This was her fury. This was her time. Nothing was going to stop her now.

As her front wheel lifted the rear squirmed on the loose-surfaced road, her smile grew. The motorcycle was a big heavy bike, not like the dirt bikes she grew up on. This was the original hooligan bike of the 1990s. The first naked street fighter that many had customised, but nothing like the weaponry her dad had fitted to this custom-build. Nobody could match the engineering prowess - or the sheer craziness - of her dad.

These roads were not the place for this bike, not its natural habitat. This bike was a handful at the best of times. Black rubber struggled to grip on the rough, pale, textured surface. As the front wheel bounced its way along, she ripped open the throttle in a moment of anger and confidence. Still leant over, with her small lightweight body clinging to the bike, the front tyre gave up. The large rear tyre pushed the front out further and its grip gave way, causing her to get her knee down for the first time. Unfortunately, her elbow, her shoulder and the entire machine followed.

The bike slid along the ground. Dust began to fill her helmet, impregnating her lungs with the dirt of the road. Heat and pain burned in to her, until the bike came to a gradual stop and Dani finally released her Pit Bull grip of the handle bars. The delicate but perfect frame of Dani fell sideways to the ground in a final thud.

A frustration grew inside her clouded mind. She was unable to comprehend that her riding skills could have let her down. She could not conceive that she had made a mistake. Dragging a scuffed leg from underneath the Streetfighter, she cursed and swore.

"For fuck's sake! Shitty, fuckin' roads!"

Her right leg stung as she tried to lift the bike back onto its wheels. The pain raced up from her ankle and bit at her knee. Dropping the bike down again, the dust circled above the tank and a smell of petrol wafted into her nose. Another motorcycle appeared to her side, lifting more debris into the air and making her lovingly restored machine look even more tragic.

Dani hated seeing her builds look dirty, but what she hated more was someone seeing her fail.

She turned her head to see Otto smiling like a Staffordshire Bull Terrier - only missing the panting tongue to complete the look. Otto sat there on his off-road café racer, with a daft grin on his face. Dani looked at him in disgust. Fearing the words he might say, she attacked first.

"What the fuck is that bike? Is it a café racer or a fuckin' dirt bike? It's as confused as a politician with an honesty box."

Otto laughed as he spoke which annoyed Dani more.

"*A bike that didn't slide down the road on its side, that's what it is.*"

Under her breath she muttered all kinds of obscenities before demanding that Otto help her get the bike upright.

He obliged, as ever. He would do anything for her. His soft, gentle approach to life was fluttering through his mind. His mother had taught him respect and compassion as key values. Dani had developed hate and disgust. Dani needed a man who would fight with her, rough and tumble, giving it back as hard as she dealt it out. She was like a dog wanting to prove dominance with anyone who dared.

The bike sat on its side-stand with just minor scuffs and dents. Otto suggested bringing it back to the garage to repair it. Dani screamed at him as she tried to get more words out than humanly possible. She rushed each and every word as if it were her last.

"*Fuck this shit! I'm out of here. I have a crusade - a fuckin' mission!*"

Otto laughed and explained that one day she will realise how much he loves her and how much he just wants to care for her. Her annoyance peaked as she stormed up to him, pushing her nose against his.

"What makes you think I need caring for, Dick? I'll die before I let anyone take care of me!"

Pressing the starter button, the old carburettors gurgled fuel through the venturis. The old engine rumbled its way to idle. The rough noise excited her and it almost brought a smile to her face, as she straddled her slightly battered bike. Calm began to flow into her as the vibrations moved through her body. It was like a hug that kept her safe. The small crash did nothing to slow her down. Spinning the rear wheel and lifting the front, she left Otto with as much recklessness as ever.

Every bend was raucous and on every straight the throttle was fully open. Every road was her sanctuary. She was more like her dad than she knew. Her knowledge of old engines was perfect; she had stripped this one down to every last nut and bolt, she had tuned the carburettor by sound alone, with notes in workshop manuals left by both Morris and her dad. She felt a connection to this bike and as the pod filters sucked in air. The induction noise delighted her, thrilled her and exited her. She imagined the fuel mixing and being drawn through into the engine. She had held the jets in her hand, fettled and re-fitted the main jet, adjusted the heights to the specification of her dad. She was proud of this bike and she showed it, anyone that told her this bike was old, a workhorse or even remotely said anything negative about it, had been met with anger. A rampage of obscenities and insults, picking at the insecurities the person had, until they looked away and hung their head.

She had out raced, race rep bikes and pulled up at cafés to laugh when they finally caught her up, teasing them as they awkwardly and carefully slowly parked the expensive bikes. She would slowly undo her leather jacket exposing her breasts held in by a thin white top, just adding insult to injury and remaining untouchable. She hated the pretentious posers and hipsters. She was rough and ready in personality but had taken good care of herself. She was very much the young female version of her dad.

The loud wail of her 4 cylinder Japanese engine sang its song of delight. As she accelerated along a wide road with rolling hills and a bright red cloud, with a spattered sunset illuminated her, it brought in an odd feeling of something she did not understand. She quickly sped away from it, outrunning her grief and silencing it with her favourite internal combustion symphony.

Kicking the side stand down, with her chunky yet feminine boot her smile grew, creating the dimples she had often hated; this was the start of something amazing. Every great story she had hear about her dad started the same way and here she was in a dusty car park and with a black coffee. The waitress had picked her way across the potholed surface to bring her order to her.

"It's been a while Dani, where are you heading?"

Dani turned her head away and gave a little wink, a little smile crept over her face, revealing the small dimples again, the waitress turned and left with her empty tray and a smile that radiated from her.

The waitress skipped through the door of the café and thought to herself. How does she do that? How does she make me feel like this? Even my husband can't make me feel like this?

The cooling coffee slipped past Dani's lips, her eyes narrowed and she thought.

Why am I different? Why do I not fit in? Why did I not follow the rest of the people, the safe life? The path of many!

A deep breath flooded through her lungs and a feeling of confusion surrounded her, a feeling of regret climbed into her head, it hurt her, tortured her and tormented her. Even her double black coffee tasted weak, it was double strength as always. Nothing had tasted good for some time she revelated about her life.

Emotion had never been close to her, the sight of happiness or sadness annoyed her, she was cold, she was hardened and she was broken. All of the things she had heard Indy and Jack discuss about her dad, overhearing phrases when they thought she was not listening, *two peas in a pod them, she is a mini Dan.* The only person who had changed Dan was her mum, the thought pained her, ripped at her heart causing physical pain in her to build into her head, dragging with it a sickness that crept up into her mouth. This was the wonderful woman they all talked about, the wonderful mum she had no memory off.

She had no memories of either of them, no happy birthdays or happy Christmases from them. Not even a well done from them when she did anything well. Indy was lovely, a great parent, nobody would have been sad to have Indy as a mum. Unless all you craved were your real parents like Dani did.

The perils of life, damaged by others, damaged by actions you had no control over. These thoughts tied her up, Dani needed pain, it was the only friend she knew, she often felt like she was going insane, the only familiar feeling was the anguish that ripped a hole into her soul.

The more pain she dealt with the more she found. Pain had become a drug for her but had left her cold. As she finished the remains of her coffee she thought deeper than ever before. As I stand here with the sun dropping behind me. Who am I? Who should I be?

Hanging upside down and twisted inside out, I could find a million pounds right now and none of that would matter. Why?

A laboured breath was slowly rippling it way out, her feeling mixed. Her answers flooded into her mind. Dark feelings. Horrible feelings. Feelings no one should have to battle with. She wanted to die, she had seen Indy suffer with those dark thoughts, she knew the signs. These signs hit her hard. She was suffering and this was her time. She looked to her side, the death machine her dad had customised, the perfect machine to do the deed with. My time is now.

Dani's thoughts cramped in her stomach, she had barley eaten in days. Her mind had been swimming in darkness for some time now, she had no idea how broken she had become.

An odd feeling rose up from her pained stomach and gathered in her throat.

Feeling this was new, something she had no understanding off. She swallowed hard and gathered her mind, stood up straight; this was her day, her day to do the deed.

The waitress shouted across at Dani, her voice echoed across the carpark, happiness bouncing of everything it touched.

"Are you staying? There are rooms still next door. Surly now the sun has set its time for a different type of drink?"

The cute feminine voice stopped her thoughts, silenced the demons and brought her back to the dusty car park with a bump. She wheeled her bike around the back and parked under a makeshift shelter that the owner someone had built for weary bikers.

Stepping into the room with the waitress felt eerily strange, it felt familiar yet not. She only knew Valentina's name from her name tag, she had been to the café next door many times over the years.

"Dani, do you like girls? I know that sounds odd and I don't know why I feel like this, my husband has always made me happy, but for some reason I, I just feel different when I see you. You are pretty yet have a masculine air about you, a look that could charm the birds from the trees with just raise of your delicate hand, or kill a man without a second thought."

The words startled Dani, the words caught her off guard. Kill a man she thought, no kill a woman, not just any woman. Tania! The evil in her soul had risen and she felt alive, she felt hope, it poked a small hole in her blackened mind. I need to avenge my Dad, avenge my mother. I need to rid this world of any corruption or greed. Her thoughts trampled through her mind as she stood motionless and emotionless. This is it time to stand proud and be counted. I am going to make my mark in this world like my Dad would have wanted.

Valetina was looking at her feet and mumbling a sorry. Dani smiled, lifted up Valentina's chin with a single delicate finger. She looked deep in her eyes and kissed her on her forehead.

"You wear a wedding ring and speak of your husband. I have no idea what we may have done next, but either your husband is here to share it or we do nothing. The world has enough pain in it, we don't need to add to it. Go home make love to your husband and hold him close, we all need a little love."

With a peal of wisdom given, the thought of living by her morals fluttered through her soul. Tearing through the dusty car park, the darkness was filled the exhaust noise and the smell of an old petrol bike, as the dust settled she was gone into the night with Valentine sat in her car, sending a sexy selfie to her husband with the message. On way home, my pants were so wet I have taken them off, I will be home in 10 mins xxx.

With Valentia on her way to make love to her husband, Dani was on her way to rid the world of evil, thinking of all the hurt and hatred she had seen. The feelings bubbled up from the blackened depths of her mind. A memory of a list she had found in one of her dads leather jackets, a list of corruption that upset him. Dani had found many lists from her dad, mainly to do lists, however this one was different, some were crossed off, however many were not.

The list had been carried by her dad for many miles, she was now carrying them close to her chest too. The list was long and detailed, full of examples of people and companies that had caused atrocities. The directory was full of unhappiness scrawled across its pages, which was now seeping in to her heart.

She hated the world. Only dipping her toe in when needed, steering away from the masses. The moral and cultural decline, hurt her. She was spurred on by comments of, *just like your dad you are*. She particularly hated the excessive destructive self-indulgence of modern society. Indy had told her many times, listing to Dani was like hearing her dads voice, she had never know what to do with these words of good intent from Indy, she was proud to be like her dad, but despised that she had no memories of him, just stories from all those that had been around before, Tania ruined her life.

Indy had visited many people over the years with Dani and they all spoke fondly of her dad, but no one realised it pained her to hear and not know first-hand who he was, not to know what his hug would have been like, not to know what joys she would have had learning from him, not to know the sanctuary only her dad could have brought. .

Trees came and fields went. Shades of colours filled the skies as she tried to outrun her past. The faster she went the faster it chased. History rode on the pillion seat tapping on her shoulder, yet she felt calm as she rode alone. A peace was with her as she flowed from apex to apex. Playing with her tyres and allowing her bike to rest on the edge of their grip. Smiles filled the helmet and the pain slipped away, no thoughts in her mind only happiness. For the bike was her pleasure, her mother and her father. It was a link to everything she wanted and the only way she knew to settle her unsettled feelings.

Many roads and vistas had melted into the past, she was weary and the sun had risen and was now falling once again in the sky, the warmth of it slowly fading and the sky now crimson. The sunsets and sun rises intrigued her, a romantic notion of writers sitting in nature creating their world pleased her.

Indy had schooled her well, Dani was well educated. Sharper than Dan, sharper than Joanne, she was a mix of both of them with a hint of Indy. She was all three of them.

Her exhaust note bounced of the building as the darkness came. The reverberations bounced from art deco building to Baroque. Lavish details sparkled in the reflections of the water, 300 miles had passed as she sat on a bench, with her feet crossed, she balanced them on the foot peg of her bike. Here she sat exhausted, alone yet surrounded by people who passed her by, none of the peaked any interest for her. She enjoyed the solitude, she craved it but she was always curious. Intrigued by people, the way they move the things they do. Behaviour watching was a hobby for Dani and the cities provided that in abundance.

Revelating at the people, this was the ideal place, this beautiful city with a dark underbelly carrying a history of both pain and beauty. It was a place that had always spoke to her, the contrasting splendour was overshadowed often by the revellers that come here for their fix, exploring their vices and allowing themselves to explore who they really are.

Amsterdam was truly a city of two halves. Cosmopolitan people and the hippies, with everyone else caught somewhere in between.

Why was she here? What did she want? What was she going to do with the list? And more importantly what was her plan for Tania? The questions were basic to her and the more she revelated the deeper they became.

What would she become? Would she end up like her dad? Who was he? Was he good or bad? What is good and bad? Was Tania doing her job or was Dan's job to rid this world of the nasty self-righteous people? Who decides what is right or wrong?

The thoughts were now tearing her mind apart, gone was the sanctuary of riding her bike and back was the need to avenge her dad. Finish his life for him. She needed to give him peace before she could settle in to her life and decide what she wanted.

As she sat in her own little world, she felt a familiar feeling and she allowed it to wash over her, the thoughts in her mind began to slow. *I am never lonely when I am alone, I am however lonely in groups of people, the bigger the crowd the more lonely I feel.*

Looking at the list she had taken from her inside pocket, the lights appeared to flicker from the water bouncing of her eyes as they stared at the words on the page. The list had niggled at her for years.

Why had my dad wrote this list? Would he have actually acted up on it? Was it just therapy? She mused on these questions, was this list actually ever going to be ticked off or was it just a way of emptying painful thoughts from a struggling mind. She had read more psychology books than most doctors, the rational side of her believed her dad was just exercising his demons, however the irrational side said it was a to do list. Indy had always said it was nothing but a rant, a way to make sense of it all. Indy was pure. Indy was sweet. Indy was innocent. Dan was none of those things, his morals where always very strong in his heart but only for his beliefs and for his specific way of thinking. His honour meant more to him than anything else. These thoughts wandered around her mind as she turned an old key in the lock of a weathered door. A place Indy had brought her many times. The cold and slightly damp air hit her as she pushed her bike through the large double doors.

She perused the list while she sat on an old dusty wing back chair, she knew what she wanted to do. It was all very clear in her mind, her dad wanted revenge, she had tried to suppress it often. All the stories of her dad were of a man with morals who would not tolerate people whose morals were questionable. It was time to show the world what her dad wanted to show.

CHAPTER 2: THE RAGGED EDGE OF LIFE

Sunshine shone slightly through the thin, aged and ragged curtains, which hung from the large window adorned with leaded details. The morning light illuminated her face and that was enough to awaken her. The day had started as normal, first light and Dani was awake as always. With a very quick freshen up in an old mottled white Belfast sink, with just a small amount of warm water from the kettle and she was already pushing the bike out of the front door, thinking of hot black coffee.

The boat was waiting and passengers were already boarding. Vast arrays of tourists were gathered at the end of a visit to Amsterdam. Some dressed in tweed and wearing very arty type clothes, some dressed in hippy trippy clothes, but many dressed in tracksuits and hoods. With her bike loaded and bags secured Dani settled, her mind was focussed and sharp. On board the boat she desired to be incognito, drift away with no one able to notice her. She looked at the beauty which surrounded her and saw the scum of society. The view towards land showed what was left form the night before. A girl sat on a bench with smudged make up and messy hair, the groups of lads shouting and pointing at her trying to intimidate the lonely confused young woman.

A friendly yet stern voice floated from the tannoy, announcing the boats departure. Dani sat back in her chair in the small breakfast area…it was going to be a long day. Pain had to be avenged.

The food barley registered as she stared along the boat's view, looking passed everyone, seeing nothing. A sip of her hot black beverage dragged her back to the reality she sat in.

She eyed a tall man, with defined shoulders and v shaped torso. His pert bum bulged as he shifted from foot to foot. Dani was never sure of her sexuality. Dani could never decide on who excited her. This man clearly had. The feelings of excitement rushed in her stomach a feeling of desire flooded through her body, but stoic she remained. A sip of her steaming brew intensified the feeling as she felt a desire to take him there and then…regardless of who might see.

Taking a deep breath, the thoughts tried to regain control. The stoic Dani argued with the impulsive Dani and a feeling of unsettled and unresolved desire bubbled inside her.

Completely unaware of her surroundings, or the people around her, a man in an expensive suit sat beside her without intruding himself.

"Do you mind if I join you?"

Dani's face spoke before she could make any response, the man smiled and explained

"No need to worry, maybe I can help you and you can help me?"

"Help me! Who the fuck do you think you are! Help me! What makes you think I need help?"

Her face was harsh; her eye makeup extenuated the harsh look with very little effort. Aggressive dark eye liner, creating wings on both eyes, thick and bold, they completed the look, with only a hint of red under the eyebrow.

Dani could not stand when men perceived her as needing any form of help, she barley ever asked for either. The man introduced himself as Dave and was well spoken, with an undertone of a Manchester scally. He explained if she would take a package on her bike, he would pay her well. He placed bundle of money on the table and told her here is five hundred and another 3 large when you drop off the package in the North for me.

Nonchalantly she picked up her cup and took a large sip, never once breaking eye contact. The escapism from her favourite morning ritual teased its way between her tight pursed lips. Her heart race increased, but no tell was shown on her face. Her blood was superheated and her mind exploded with words she wanted to say. None of the words were allowed to come. None of them bubbled out, what she did allow out was her hot coffee, she spat the entire mouthful in the man face.

"Fuck you!"

Dave was unable to remain calm he leapt across at her and grabbed her by the throat. Her slender figure and weight was no match for him. The large hand had wrapped easily around her throat and he pinned her to her seat, searing pain into her back. The smell of the coffee trickled into her nostrils. A small smirk forced its way across her face. The pressure from his hand caused pain to burn into her mind. Once again, she refused to acknowledge her disadvantaged position. She was never ready to admit she had lost.

Dave let out a pained breath as she drove her fork between his legs. Forcing it harder and harder until she could make no more depth with the fork, then she twisted it and he fell to the ground with bulging red eyes and saliva splattering all over the deck as he screwed his face up in agony.

Dani's stoic face returned, in full control of herself, she knelt down beside him.

"Don't fuck with me; you have no idea who I am!"

A secret smile filled her internally as she felt the rage and power mix. She possessed a rare skill. An ability to be completely out of control internally yet, calm to the outside world.

Calmly she stared at him, calmly she stroked his face and calmly she plotted killing him. He was a drug runner, praying on vulnerable runaways and trying to entice them to take all the risk, to run county lines. Fuckin' scum she thought, he is going on the list she thought. The thoughts unravelled in her head, he is ruining the lives of the people who are lost, the people who need saving, the people who have nothing left to lose.

Torturous thoughts drowned her mind and nothing around her was in focus. Her dark mind exploded with, *he is going overboard.* He had to be removed from society, ticked off the list. It's what Dan would have done!

Dave dragged himself to his knees clutching his testicles, Dani stood stern and solid, he controlled the splitting pain he felt and said one word, a word that literally knocked her back into her seat.

"Dan."

Wide eyed and reeling from the shock, how could this man know my dad? She crumbled from the hard bitch to a feeling of a little girl who needed to be scooped up by her father and protected. The feeling shook her entire being. She stood back up from her chair, her legs felt weak and wobbly, her stomach contorted, and a sickness filled her. Who was this? How did he know my dad's name? Her stride was as confident as she could be, but confident she was not, she strode away and scowled over her shoulder. Escape was the only thing she needed, her bike was her desire, she needed to flee.

Pacing back and forth stepping from foot to foot, looking unsettled, she had no idea what she had done or who she had met, as the bike was un-tethered, she hurriedly went to it, pushing her way past people. She gently rotated the old-fashioned choke, started the bike and the rich petrol fumes filled the air. A momentarily safe feeling surrounded her. Her feelings of fear were silenced by the exhaust noise which reverberated of the walls inside the ferry.

She had been told many times by Jack as they had departed from many boats, often with her on the back of his bike, that the departure ramps were slippery.

The unsettled thought was silenced but still running around inside her head, shaken she rode down towards the tarmac. As soon as her wheels touched the safety of the road, she accelerated and the loud and less than discreet departure turned the heads of everyone, including Dave who now stood on the deck taking a picture of her departure. The caption below the picture read, looks whose back from the dead.

Questions swirled around her caffeinated brain, as she tried to make sense of her world.

"Where next? What Next? Who next"

Answers flooded in. I have so many problems and not enough time, so many negative thoughts so deal with and so many negative people to deal with. Wind rushed around her delicate torso, a tight-fitting leather jacket that was well worn around the edges with tight jeans that had seen much sunshine. Both of these had seen a couple of low-speed slides. The ragged look often helped her get what she wanted from people, she was stunning even without even trying to be.

Dani had learnt how easy manipulation of people was, particularly men. She had learned how to control people by her words, her actions, and her looks. Did this make her bad ass and clever? Or did this make her damaged and a narcissist? Who could tell who would care? Dani had a purpose, a set of plans and much fuckery to cause. Dani had no fear of society apart from ending up part of it.

Sun flicked into her visor as she enjoyed herself, overtaking cars on her back wheel, narrowly missing oncoming traffic and squeezing back into the correct lane. Dani had nothing to lose as she had nothing. Her soul was empty, her life was empty and her happiness was empty. Life had nothing to offer, life was a one-way ticket of adrenaline and fear mixing to together to fill a void in her heart. She was a natural reaction to a fucked up situation. Apparently it was some personality disorder that she had refused to work with a therapist over. Jack had set it up for her and all she wanted to do was see the world burn for her pain.

There are many places to be, who will remember me? Why will they remember me? What will they say about me? Dani's thoughts stamped wildly, around her mind. *No one can tell me what to do. I can't be caged. I must be free to do what I want to do! I am me and that can't be changed. I am here to set the record straight. I will avenge the world and set them all free.*

Love had never felt close to Dani, she had pushed it away, Indy always took it badly, but Dani could not stay with her any longer, fighting against her desire to be free, wild and alone. Her thoughts bubbled. *I have seen enough people in my rear-view mirrors today, that's enough social interaction for me today.*

Riding recklessly was her only content and her excitement, her freedom and her solitude. A calmness settled in as she settled into her ride. One last thought bobbed in her melee of ideas around her desire to escape the world and go rouge. *You are alone now, just how you like it.*

She had waited all her life for this moment, her feelings were high as she stepped forward into the light. She was now to be the star in her own life. Indy chanted this almost daily back in Harz, never did Indy think that it would breed such hate, Indy wanted to bring her peace, love and happiness. What Dani took was hate, discontent and resentment.

The light faded and so did her calmness, the list she had in her jacket burned its way from her inside pocket into her mind. The list danced around her head tormenting her. How long could she hold it together? Where she was heading, was too far to get to before dark. Her mind was now a wash with memories, a wash with her childhood pains. The pains were dark as she bounced along a farm track, dust and dirt spitting up from her tyres as she headed off road.

Dani was hardened by her life, she was strong and only needed a quiet space to layout her roll mat and sleeping bag. Where she was strong against the elements, she was not strong mentally. No one would believe the weakness she hid from everyone. Her mind was constantly one small step away from either rage or tears.

Settling down next to the bike, the grass was soft and fragrant. Wild flowers circled her, the smells twirled around in her nostrils; it felt like a safety net as the sun dropped. Avoiding her thoughts was always difficult, her own worst enemy awoke, her brain was taking charge as she closed her eyes. A troubled life, pain of yesteryear and worry for tomorrow came into a hazy myriad of depression and anxiety. Living in anything but the present, her mind assaulted her with ghosts of the past and images of the future.

Dani screwed up her face, pulled her knees up tight and tried to battle the demons she carried with her. Darkness pushed its way into her face, opened her eyes and spoke to her. Voices she could not hide from came to the forefront. Visons of her troubles with Indy set in and the pain consumed her as she tried to hide. She had once saved Indy. Saved her when she was too young to understand the pain she saw in Indy, this pain attached itself to her.

Indy never got over the death of Dan, never got over what she had done to the world, the ripple effects she had caused. The anguish of being guilty of murder and seeing her true love murdered never left her. Dani had found her in a drunken stupor with a scarf around her neck and tears in her eyes, as she stood tying it to a wooden beam in the house, the sight of Dani watching her and listening to her cried chants, stopped her from ever trying that again.

Pain sat heavy in her heart. Dani tried to hide from her memories as they were served up one by one. Seeing Indy ready to leave this world with red teary eyes and cries of *I can't go on,* rang in her mind, teasing her, adding to her loaded mind. Indy had explained how she was plagued with guilt, plagued with fear and plagued with worry. Dani had only been in her very early teens when she cut the scarf from around Indy's neck and begged her never to leave her, never to try this again and never to get so low again. This moment changed everything; this moment put Dani in the parent role, counselling Indy, helping her grow.

Feelings of sorrow were triggered in Dani and from this day she was never the same again.

Begging Indy to stay had unleashed the full story from Indy of her troubles, a story explaining how she had been found by Ritchie in a room doing the same and he had saved her. He had sat with her until Dan arrived. The stories were difficult to hear, changing a young innocent mind into a broken and hardened state. Dani hand spent many evenings supporting Indy when actually Dani her self-needed support.

Reflecting on her parents' death had worn a young innocent mind down, she had no memories of them but the stories.

All those years ago, a cold day had seen Jack personally gather many people together, the rain beat down on them as they rode with the two coffins of her parents in a hearse, Indy and Dani rode in a side car following at the back. Many bikers with no helmets rode along spraying up rooster tails of rain from bobbed bikes, bullet like rain drops bounced of many bald heads. Wet leathers and shivering bikers all stood at the crematorium with rain pouring heavily in muddy puddles and big boots, stood sinking in to the wet grass, to pay respect to them. Jack had always explained how significant Dan had been. Jack had arranged everything including the emotional speech he gave, swallowing deeply has he fought back tears. A strong voice echoed around the crematorium, that occasionally croaked with emotion, before he regained his composure and continued with his words. He told a story of many hardened bikers stood silently subdued at the crematorium, male and female all stood with an eerie silence around them apart from the fait crying of Indy. She recited the speech from Jack in her sleep still to this day.

Our brother and sister who rode for everyone, fought their own cause and still gave everything to all they met.

Two people who were taken from this world and who cannot be replaced.

Two people who will never leave my heart.

Two people who touched my soul.

Two people I am proud to call brother and sister.

May Odin take them in to the hall of slain warriors.

May Odin look after them in the palace roofed with shields, allowing them to feast on the flesh of fresh boar to make them whole again each evening.

The pain in Dani's head burned at the front of her thoughts, literally paining her forehead in a perfect circle, as if a hot poker was being forced into her mind.

Standing tall with the morning dew still on her face, the early sun glistened against her skin. A new dawn always pleased her, a chance to make it right, a chance to start again, a chance to forget the woes of yesterday.

Fresh from a swim in the river than ran along the edge of the woods, she was ready for her day, ready to regroup, ready to bring the revelations of hell to anyone who had crossed her father. The list was crumpled and well read, the paper was thin, aged and slightly tatty.

People who crossed me and Gluttonous People Who Have Stamped on the Common People.

- Tania

- Dotty's killer (Billy and wife)

- Drug cartel of those Indy killed in the petrol station

- Dick head weasel Tyler who knocked my phone and coffee out of my hand; Burger place in Milton Keynes

- Restoration Bike Services

- Factory owner (stole my friends pensions and other shit)

- See List on tool box too!

Carefully she folded the list up and placed in her pocket. There was a place she knew she would be welcomed, a place of sanctuary, it had been a few years since her last visit, it felt oddly like home to her, more so than the Harz mountains.

Stones, dust and debris flung up as she spun the rear wheel on her exit. No secret stealth departure, it was rarely her style. Feeling her cold tyres losing traction as she entered the first tarmacked bend excited her, she spun a rear wheel as she cornered, the edge of the tyre feathered and shredded. It was a melted wave of ecstasy for her.

A moment of content appeared as she approached a lone biker, a 'race rep' one piece leather wearing type, a feeling of desire mixed with a feeling of dominance. Dani played with people like they were toys more often than anyone else she had ever met.

She edged her bike along the inside of his on the next right-hand bend, undertaking him enough to be seen. Backing off and doing the same on the next left-hand bend, her bike at one with her. A completely zen type feeling inside her took over as she continued to push harder and harder. The Race bike's cross plane crank noise boomed from the exhaust. Racing a new faster better bike was her favourite taunt, until the rider in front's bravery on the straight road came. The biker opened the throttle and the faster more superior bike accelerated away from her, she smiled as the biker's brake light glowed and the nose of the bike dived, completely off line it struggled to make the next bend, almost mounting the grass verge on one side and crossing the white line on the next. Dani accelerated towards the bike as the race replica bike accelerated into the next corner, Dani came in hot sliding her rear wheel, spitting stones and rubber at the fancy painted fairings of the victim. A blip of the throttle as she straightened up the bike and a tug on the bars, Dani lifted her front wheel and rode off in front chuckling about a rider with all the gear who had no idea how to ride. A happy thought rippled through her mind, *overtaken by a girl on an old bike.*

Downshifting and bouncing the revs up and down, pops bangs and flames coming from the exhaust. A delight flickered inside her, the bike felt most alive to her on downshift, pleasing her, allowing a momentary light of happiness in her darkness.

The noise of the bike still resonating in her mind and she parked in a lay-by check the map, Dani recognised the area and knew she was not far from her place of refuge.

From the distance a howling engine approached as she stood next to her bike, high in the rev range and playing the music she loved, each gear added more melody. The red and white blur approached, the front tyre struggled for grip and overshot the layby with the front brake pulled as hard as possible. She watched intently as the large biker backed the bike into the lay-by. Leaping from the bike, the rider almost ripped his helmet off, threw it wildly to the ground. A clean-cut boyish face was revealed on an overweight man in brand new leathers, he left his huge shiny new machine pinging as the parts started to cool down.

Anger and hate radiated from his face, screwed up adding lines to his young face. He was already shouting and bounding towards her.

"Fucking bitch, you could have killed us both!"

Hairs stood up on the back of her neck as he pushed his face into hers. She hated people pushing into her space, especially close to her face.

"If you could ride faster than an O.A.P. I would not have had to fuck with you!"

Immediately his temper was bristled, a dented ego on a young man with a sports bike, told by a petite girl on an old bike, he was not able to ride fast, just elevated his rage. He forced her to the ground and leant his body weight against her with his huge forearm. Pressure mounted against her delicate throat as she struggled for breath.

"Fuckin' split arse, you're fukin' dangerous, I bet that piece of shit isn't even your bike, old man's bike that!"

With that he reached down and forced his hand between her legs, pulling at the zip on her trousers, telling her, he will teach her a lesson, show you what a real man is like.

Lay in the dirt of the lay-by on a back country road, she knew she had to think fast, he was easily nearly double her weight. She was still holding the rock and the penknife she had been sharpening it on, she calmly and slowly reached her hand up and stabbed straight through his leathers, piercing the crotch and into his testicles. Screams and spit showered her face as the fat man in leathers rolled around on the floor. Blood was already filling his pants and seeping into his hands.

Dani slowly stood up. She rubbed her throat with one hand as she slowly walked over to where the fat man now lay mooing like a wounded cow. A sneer wrinkled her nose as she looked at him in disgust. Her stomach tightened and her teeth clenched. She felt the disgust for him explode inside her.

"Just because I am a woman, don't make me easy...I am not your property! Is this how you prove you manliness? Which woman laughed at you? Which woman told you your pin dick didn't even touch the sides?"

She kicked him square in the face. Now with one knee gently rested beside him and her arm rested on her other. She leant over him as he clutched his groin shouting how he would kill her. She slowly pushed the penknife into his throat and removed his Adams apple, leaving him coughing and spluttering to bleed out in the lay-by.

A leather clad man all in black stood amongst the trees the other side, with his helmet still on, watching it all unfold, hidden by the low branches, he nodded repeatedly to himself as she rode away, slowly and precisely. A mixed feeling of vulnerability and God complex filled her mind.

CHAPTER 3: MEMORIES I NEVER HAD

Blood now drying on her leather jacket and a large building looming into view, it was the place she had been looking for. The sight of it filled her with content. The sanctuary of bikers, the place she had visited many times, the place Dan, Joanne, Indy and Jack had all stayed before she was born. The thought of entering the building gave a small flame of happiness, but a melancholy feeling shrouded it. The air smelled of greenery and a smattering of oil. As she rolled up to the door Ritchie was in the car park, doing wheelies on an old 125cc scooter, scraping the number plate on the ground, he was chuckling like a schoolboy doing stunts on a BMX.

With her bike parked neatly as she always did, Ritchie slid the scooter around the rear of her bike, spinning the rear wheel and almost dropping it on the floor, still laughing as he put a foot down to stop himself falling off.

Howdy partner, Ritchie exclaimed with a huge boyish smile lighting up his face, he was met with a stern steely gaze as she lifted her helmet off, her hair fell slightly to the side and her eyes were cold.

"You ok? Where's Indy?"

Worry was already rumbling around his thoughts, Dani looked distant, more distant than usual. No expression and a dried red stain on her hands was revealed as she took of her gloves.

"Time we went inside I think, bring that bike too."

Moving the bike inside, she saw huge black bike on a plinth, filling a window at the front of the workshop. She immediately adored the large old school cruiser, lots of blacked out parts and some shiny chrome accenting the look. Dani asked if it is Ritchie's and a tear formed in his eyes. Emotion reddened his face and made him swallow hard to fight back the tears, the smell of two stroke oil hung in the air, the usual feeling of happiness for this fragrance was not there. In a wavy and croaky voice, he explained. That bike was your dad's black behemoth. The bike he terrorised the UK on all those years ago, starting a convoy and upsetting Scotland Yard as he set about his path of destruction. Dan had a black mood at that time, darker than his bike.

Ritchie had recovered it from the river and rebuilt it. Now it runs just like it did when Dan owned it. He had tried to ride it but every time he tried; he didn't feel it was his right to ride it.

A pain in Dani's stomach knotted up and a coldness wriggled over her body, she did not cry but felt as if she had been kicked in her gut. Ritchie started the bike up and gestured for her to sit on it. The bike made the floor shake as she threw a leg over it. The vibrations of the engine flowed into her soul, it's the closest she had ever felt to a hug from her dad, the bike he rode when he met my mum she thought, the bike he loved. His first choice for a bike was this one. His mood dressed in black and chrome. Her gaze dropped as she sunk into a world she never experienced, memories she never had, memories she wished she had, wishing she could remember him teaching her, loving her cradling her when she was young. Suddenly she was startled by the words that bounced of her shield of pain.

"Take it for a ride…it's technically your bike"

Dani looked up and gave him a wry smile. She put the bike in gear and revved the engine slightly, then hit the kill switch, she hung her head.

"No one else should ever ride this bike, this bike is my mum and dad's bike, it's their love, their happiness, it was Genesis for my mum, a phoenix moment when she met my dad…I am not yet worthy to ride it. One day I will be worthy, but not yet"

Dani got off the bike and smiled. A fake smile that she had practiced many times to shield herself from questions she did not want to answer. Ritchie immediately saw through it. His love and admiration for her wouldn't let him embarrass her, not challenging her for it, he had seen the pain she carried and seen a man carry pain in the same way before her. He had seen the same expression on her dad's face when he tried to hide his darkness, could she actually be him? Did his soul join hers in those final minutes?

Dani shared so many traits with her dad, she often said similar phrases but more eerily she had the same harsh ability to bring a person down, with one swooping phrase in a cutting voice that no one else could match. She was the female version of her dad alright, but with the beauty of her mum. If only she had more of her mum's kindness, she would be the perfect woman Ritchie thought, she was 22 years his junior but she always blew him away when she walked in the room. Her confidence was that of a 40 year old but the body of a 20 year old. Ritchie drifted off in his mind imaging Dani and what she might look like in her 40's.

He was brought back to reality with a cutting voice from Dani.

"Is this the two bikes you mentioned?"

"If you liked the Black Behemoth you are going to love these two"

He took a black and gold embroidered cover from a bike, slowly uncovering the triple twister that Morris built Dan,

Dani did not recognise the bike, she squinted as Ritchie pointed to the plaque on the frame, riveted on was the message from Morris to Dan. She touched the plaque, running her fingers over the letters, she swallowed hard and the knot in her stomach became excruciating, then the tears formed in her eyes as she turned her head away and paced until they had gone. She had not cried since she was a babe in arms, she hated it, despised the feeling of weakness. Indy had told her many times it was not weak to cry and it does you good to have a good cry. Dani had always sneered at those words, loathed and detested them.

"I have only ever cleaned it and started it, just like Dan would have asked, he started all bikes regularly. He checked them over like a sergeant inspecting a regiment"

Her breaths quickened as she saw the beauty of the bike and the gold plaque on the frame, the last bike her dad rode was in front of her, with the death machine she arrived on too, it was the start the middle and the end of her dad's life laid in front of her the three most important bikes of his.

She shifted awkwardly from side to side as she tried to imagine what her dad would have been like with these bikes, what he would have said to her and how he would have brought her up. The thoughts distorted her inside. No outward emotion left in her face, just a cold long stare. She felt the pain, it poked at her and tore a hole she could not see. She ran her long delicate fingers along the plaque once again as if was brail, feeling every groove of the engraved letters, they were rough to the fingertips and she loved the metallic feeling it gave. The neatness of the writing excited her equally as the rough texture of the engraving did.

She questioned Ritchie, asking if Morris had handwritten this. The reply turned her head away as she felt an unfamiliar feeling gurgling inside her. With the feeling swallowed and an obligatory deep breath taken she was back to the steely hard glazed expression.

Ritchie nodded with his lips pursed, answering her questions without words. Allowing her to know she was right, until he pulled the sheet of one final bike.

She gasped loudly as she saw the next bike he unveiled, the tears formed again in her eyes, it was the first time he had seen emotion in her eyes, the first time she had reacted like a person would be expected to.

"This is the bike you built for me? So you can have all three of my Dad's bike on display?"

More nods were given, the feeling in the air thick, he was giving her a bike he had subtly customised for her, for free. However the stories that were told of Dan were of these three bikes, the epic tales of a renegade who gave no fucks. He looked down at his smart trainers and said softly.

"It would be an honour to have all three on display here. He is a legend in these parts, people still talk about him up and down the country too, they do motorbike tours just to go to all the places he went. They all come here and ask to see the bikes...just one bike missing and that's the old Bandit death machine"

A mix of excitement and horror tumbled through her as she thought about it. She explained she had only one condition, I will take this gold lettered triple so long as I can come back at any time and ride them bikes and no one else ever rides them. She felt as if she was in control, owning the situation. In reality Ritchie had known how to play this situation. He had no malice in mind. He actually wanted her to have her own bike and didn't need for money these days. He was completely truthful when he had said it would be an honour. He was going to continue to keep her dads name alive in the hearts of the biking community.

Sunshine smiled over his face a delight enchanted him, he was as big a fan of Dan as anyone, possibly one of his biggest fans. The pleasure was really his to store these bikes and talk about him to all the Dan wannabe's.

Wheeling the white triple twisted machine backwards she looked down at the clocks, there were no miles on the counter, all zeros. She quizzed Ritchie on how this could be.

He slowly looked at his shoes and began to tell her a story, a story of wandering around his workshop with Dan's bikes restored and still feeling like he was missing something. The day Indy had brought Dani to visit at 5 years old, he started building a bike for her with a brand new bike as the base. A bike just like the one Morris built for her dad. This one had some small neat touches for her to notice as she gazed upon it later. He had picked white as he hoped her life would not be blighted with darkness like her fathers.

"Dani before you go, look on the frame"

A brass plaque was fitted, simply saying 'Just like you dad would have wanted'. She looked at Ritchie with a stern steely gaze and slowly allowed one corner of her mouth to raise, the tiniest of smiles, but he saw it and winked at her.

"Your Dad would be proud of you."

Nodding in his general direction like one old biker passing another. She pulled on her helmet and shouted.

"ROAD TEST"

On her return the exhausts popped and cracked as she rolled in to the workshop, she sat for a moment with visor still down and a huge smile hidden away. The bike was perfect for her, she preferred the road biased bikes, not like the one that idiot Otto had built she thought. Knobbly tyres are for old men, she mused.

She loved the triple engine, loved the bark, loved the wheelie machine it was, the ultimate gift to her, it was a prize bike and her heart lifted in her chest.

"One day I will ride that behemoth, one day I will be worthy of a ride on that bike."

With her new bike parked next to the plinth in the window, Ritchie smiled at her as he pushed the death machine of her dad's up onto the mini stage to join the other two bikes. His heart skipped a beat, on loan to him maybe, but in his workshop for him to adore defiantly.

Dani wandered in between all three, silently absorbing their beauty as if they were fine art, hanging in a gallery. Each one spoke to her differently, the death machine showed a time of rage and anger, how her dad had wanted to avenge his adopted family after

Dotty was murdered. The behemoth demonstrating his no fucks to the world and his stunning triple with knobbly tyres, which looked heavily abused. The triple with knobbly tyres showed his need to be ready for anything.

With her bike parked below them, it was a moment with her father, a moment she was close to him, touching the bars he had held and showing him her bike, the white and gold triple was a tribute to him, it was her bike. It was similar to his and yet different all at once.

Ritchie placed a hand on her shoulder and she pushed him away violently like she did anyone who was kind to her, he turned and stepped away, his voice quivered and a tear rolled down his face. He had seen Dan react like that many times to many people.

"You Know Dani, I saw both Dan and Jack cry in this very room. Big tough men with a reality more scary than the image they portrayed. They both cried here and they both started to heal here too."

He tried to explain what Dan had told him. Crying is no shame, crying is good, he told of how Dan had said to him; it's something to do with endosystems I think he said, something in the body that needs to be purged by crying. Purging the pain from our bodies, Dan had explained it far better than Ritchie ever could.

"It helped me, your dad had a way of getting everyone to face the revelations of their own mind and be a better person because of it"

Tears now filled her red blood shot eyes, almost bubbling out and down her face.

"You are clearly in pain, you need to do whatever it is that helps you, but do it fast before what's in your head destroys you"

She cried and she wailed to be left alone, Ritchie pulled out a hip flask from his pocket, He told her how he found it in the bag on the behemoth.

"It's now clean and full of single malt; I have carried it for years I don't know why, maybe ready for a moment like this".

He tossed her the hip flask and told her he would be upstairs if she needed him.

The room down there is always for Indy, the one at the top of the stairs is your mum and dad's room, stay as long or as short as you need, even an acquaintance of Dan and Joanne is welcome here let alone his only daughter!

She cried for hours and Ritchie listened, not knowing what to do, but wait and be there if she needed him. She was Dan's daughter, 20 years Ritchie's junior but it felt like Dan was in the room as soon as she spoke.

The next morning she left on the white triple, leaving the streetfighter behind, it was not a bike to get seen on, her dad's streetfighter would always draw a crowd. Ritchie had told her that Tania can still be seen at bike meets. Tania continued to look for Indy to see if she returned. Tania had visited Ritchie a few times over the years, to try and find out if anyone had seen Indy or Dani.

Ritchie never mentioned to Tania, the secret visits that Indy had with Dani to his place. Tania had a list in her phone of people, the only people left alive surrounding Dan's memory and at the top of that list was Dani and Indy.

Dan had really gotten under the skin of Tania and Dani represented him, Indy fled with Dani, stopping Tania from killing them all. Tania's list was not completed. Retired or not, she was always looking for them both.

Dani pulled out her own list, the one she had found in a notepad in a leather jacket pocket hung in the garage at home, she didn't know all the names on the list but she knew they meant something to her dad. Over the years she had teased explanations on all the names from Indy. Indy had tried to ignore her, tried to take it from her, but was met with a rage bigger than Dan had ever displayed. She was harsh as Dan with the spirit of Joanne, it scared Indy many times, reduced her to tears, weeping which Dani has shouted at her over. Dani now had experienced the feeling of emotion, she wasn't comfortable with it, but tears and single malt had appeared to lighten her mental load.

A single ray of light illuminated her early morning slumber, the sun was not yet high in the sky, the early morning was cloudy with a faint ray of sunshine shining in to the darkness. First light was her time to leave; she always loved the crisp fresh morning, when most people were still asleep.

She placed the hip flask on the table in her room, with a scribbled note stuck to it, just what I needed, keep it full always, I will return with enough to keep us all smiling.

Quietly and quickly she rolled her new white, triple engine bike out to the road, a quick glance over her shoulder allowed her one final look at the 3 bikes in the window. She had not noticed the biker sat on the fence on the other side of the road, dressed in black and hidden by the early morning shadows. As he watched her, she started her bike and very slowly wafted away along the road allowing her engine to gently warm up. The black leathered biker was gone, returned to the shadows he came from.

CHAPTER 4: RISE OF THE BEAST

Shadows fell behind her and the sky turned from red to blue evoking an emancipated feeling wafting behind. Her new white beast of a bike thrilled her more than a bike usually did. Short wheel base and lots of torque meant the front wheel tried to lift every time she was hard on the throttle. The first few caught her by surprise, creating waves of excitement in her stomach. Now she was starting to get air on the front wheel, as she changed at the redline in second and popped it in to third. The wheel came up and her mood went with it. She immediately felt at ease. Many small little modifications had been made but nothing that immediately stood out. This was her new favourite bike. This was her new pleasure. This was her new happiness. With her peg now occasionally scraping the floor flicking up sparks on the uneven road surface. She was focused. The world had gone and all that was left was her companion. The bike.

The road showed her the way and the bike carried her with Valkyrie like happiness. She had no plans, no desires and no hate. She was in the happiest place she could imagine. Every corner an opportunity to brake late, pops and crackles fluttered behind her, just before she opened the throttle and the front wheel went light again.

Blue LED's illuminated in the rev counter in front of her, when she was high in the rev range and for most of the ride they were on constantly. This was the moment of escape, but a new light glared at her, the tank was already running dry and she needed fuel.

The old petrol station was grotty but served a purpose. Nothing in there was to her liking, even the clumsy person serving, he didn't even understand how to operate the card machine correctly. She had no intention of paying by card…that would be a real emergency, Jack had taught her that. She slammed the exact cash on the counter and the young boy jumped banging his elbow against the display next to the till, accidently knocking several sunglasses and LED torches on to the floor. Dani muttered as she so often did at people

"Fuckin' twat".

Cash left next to the card machine and she was gone before the boy even noticed. People who could not function well in her world, annoyed her, clumsiness, inept or faffing, boiled her blood. A darkness had crept back into her world. It was inside her helmet, surrounding her rage and discontent permeated through her being.

Engine started, exhausts rumbling and her list in her hand, she knew she was not far away and a name on the list could be ticked off. One she wanted so bad. One she knew would have pleased her dad to avenge. The next 25 mins were a blur of dangerous overtakes and close calls.

Side stand down and helmet balanced on her tank, she strutted away from it, she could not help but glance back, beauty and aggression in one package, gold detail and black wheels contrasting with the metallic white paint. She was smitten and a little obsessed. She ordered some food and a black coffee. Nobody really stood out, no one was remarkably different a room full of the drab, grey and dull. Nobody in this room was worth speaking too Dani thought. The description Indy had begrudgingly given her of this place, had told of a young boy with dark rimmed glasses who didn't stand up straight, fumbled around and struggled to speak. Indy had even done her own impression of Dan telling the story to her, which Dani adored.

The food was gone and her coffee nearly empty. A young girl with bright make up and colourful tattoos came over and asked if she could clear the tray away, she was sweet and articulate with an air of confidence about her. Dani's interest was piqued by her. Someone who was not as dull as the vanilla ice cream they served.

"Excuse me miss have you worked here long?"

The girl's eye role was so loud it made Dani chuckle inside, the girl explained, she had only been her a few weeks, she just needed cash to get through university.

"Does a Tyler work here? Possibly worked here a very long time"

An even louder eye role was her response as she explained her shift manger was called Tyler, he had worked here so long he ended up shift manager, he couldn't manage to shift a box, let alone an entire shift of people. Dani let a small smile emerge as she requested a coffee refill and to speak with Tyler. The girl returned a few moments later and gave her another coffee.

"Tell Tyler I will be outside and I have a complaint"

Dani sat on the bench staring at her bike and sipping her cooling coffee the moment was just like any other, distanced from the world, there, yet not there. A man approached in the standard issue uniform, a vast array of company badges clipped to his shirt pocket and a goofy expression on his face. As he stepped off the kerb he tripped over his own feet and nearly fell flat on his face. He chuckled and smiled at her, this solidified her rage as she sat perfectly still, not even breathing as she looked at him, her glare made him nervous.

His greeting was sickly nice asking how he could be of assistance. A few seconds passed and Dani did not even blink, her fringe fluttered slightly in the breeze and her dreadlocked hair sat on her shoulders, it was as red as ox blood.

"My dad was in here a while back and was treated badly. I want to make a complaint"

His response was even more nice and even more sickly sweet, so much so he could have worked on kids' television program. Dani was now stood up, leaving her steaming coffee on the bench. She explained how her dad was in here ordering a drink and some fool pushed passed him while he stood in the que, the staff member did not say excuse me, just squeezed through the impossible gap in the line of people. This fool had knocked her dad's phone and cash clean out of his hand, crashing against the floor, luckily not breaking his device as he never broke a phone in his life.

Horror and astonishment appeared in his face as he asked how long ago this was.

"About 25 years ago dick face"

Apologies and flustered words bumbled out of his middle aged man's mouth, his rounded shoulders sunk from his arched forward spine, Dani was sure this was tick number one on the list. She had prepared mentally for this moment, She was stern and cold, perfectly in control of her actions. Tyler was daft. Tyler was incompetent. Tyler was clumsy. He was however not nasty. No intent. No malice. She stepped forward eyeing him nose to nose as he flustered more words, wringing his hands in front of himself. Nothing he could say would change this outcome. 25 years ago, a ripple effect had taken place all the way to this moment, this was destiny, this was an avengement, this was for Dan.

She knew he did not deserve any of this, he was just on the list and stupid needs to learn, she punched him in the stomach and doubled him over, as his head lined up with her waist, she slapped him hard on the side of the ear sending shockwaves through his ear drum, excruciating pain seared into his head straitening him up as if trying to emit the pain through the top of his skull with both hands clamped onto the side of his head. He staggered back as she leapt at his chest and dropped her elbow into his sternum, sending him reeling backwards until he fell against the railings. On lookers stood stationary, gasping. The shock hit them hard as everyone watched her calmly sip from her coffee, place her helmet and gloves on, no rush no haste, then serenely and sedately ride away. Tyler lay on the floor gasping for breath as one onlooker asked if he was okay before looking to see if she had gone.

"'Ard bitch that, you going to okay pal?"

Tyler was now choking on his own vomit with tears rolling down his cheeks and snot pouring from his nose. Nobody moved, everyone was stunned as they watched him cough and splutter on his last meal. A blue flash of heavily starched polyester fluttered passed everyone. An off duty nurse still in uniform appeared as if from nowhere. Rolling him on to his side and patting his back. He started to cry and the nurse tried to reassure him that he was okay. Tyler cried more and tried to cuddle into the nurse. She skilfully positioned herself out of his reach, this was clearly not her first rodeo. Her round bottom was now exposed from under the short blue dress, two young lads giggled while taking pictures of her sheer tights stretched across her bum exposing her underwear. The scowl from the nurse made them laugh as they started there two stroke 'peds' up a cloud of smoke wafted around them and they slurped at a milkshake still giggling like school kids.

Scenery had come and gone, blurred roads forgotten. As Dani sat on a bench watching the sun glisten off a crystal blue lake. Her senses slowly weaved their way back into her mind. She was excited, stoic on the outside but bouncing like a child at a 10th birthday party inside. Carefully removing the list of revenge her dad had written. She ticked off Tyler. It gave her an enormous sense of achievement, brightness grew inside her carrying hope and delight. A warm feeling was growing inside her, she imagined her dads hand resting on her shoulder, guiding her through life. She had started her dads work. She had avenged her dad, someone who he wished he had punished at the time. The thought had tortured him for years, someone who got away. It may have been only one person, but this feeling was consuming her, high on the addictive drug she had now found, imagining her dad being happy, that people who had done him wrong were educated on their stupidity.

Scanning her eyes along the neat and precise witting, the paper old and discoloured further pushed her emotions, chipping away at her stoic silence. The list was almost memorised and yet she still looked at it daily. The pain she carried from not having her parents around, now diverted to others. Each name on the list absorbed a small amount of her issues and brought her closer to her dad. Some of the people listed had done wrong by the common man, not put people before profits these also needed to be educated.

Questions filled her mind. *What would Dan do now? What would Indy think? Was she a hero or a villain?*

A sombre notion crept through her being, sending a cold streak through her entire body. She worried about Indy; she feared what her dad might have said about the way she had spoken to Indy. She was horrified by how awful she had treated Indy as she allowed all the thoughts of what she had done to the people that cared about her, throughout her life, to trickle into her consciousness.

The Happy Hippy had always looked after her, she had put Dani first and cared for in every way possible. A feeling Dani did not care for stirred in her thoughts and rippled through her core. *Had she thrown all that back at Indy? Had she ever said thank you for all that she had done?*

Dani turned over the old faded list, she took out her pencil and started her own list, her list of redemption. The only name she wrote came easy, the first person she had to set free was Indy. Scratching her nose with the pencil, a name or two flickered around her mind and teased her. Those other names were not ready to join the list and with that her bike was running and the white street fighter shined in the sunshine. The metallic flakes catching the light and exciting her. A crack of her throttle and she was now just a memory in Tyler's mind.

An older woman arrived and got out of a large sports car, roof down hair tied up and dark sunglasses. She wandered around the carpark with the two stroke 'peds' now leaving in a cloud of blue smoke, her footsteps clumped along in large black tactical boots, with very tight and fitted combat trousers; she looked at the small pile of sick on the floor, almost examining the content. Her small radio crackled in to life.

"Tania what do you need?"

Ice cold, she never replied, marching straight inside and grabbing the weeping Tyler by his stained uniform.

"Who was she? What did she say?"

It was the old Tania interrogating the weak man, It was the militant Tania. It was the evil Tania back again, hunting her victim. Tyler cried more as he tried to speak. Tania ordered the staff around demanding a double espresso and the CCTV. Without a thank you or any niceties. Tania was soon back in her sports car with her drink and a memory stick of the footage taken from the CCTV.

Dani had no idea that Tania had been tipped off for the incident in the car park. She meandered through her world, ghosts of her memories haunted her, shadows filled her thoughts, which tortured and tormented her. The pain she was in, tried to consume her, show her where she had gone wrong in life. Dani was used to dealing with such pain. Her thoughts were muddy and her soul filled with dark colours. She was beginning a battle big enough to be with Satan himself.

Why did I hurt Indy so much? Why did I cause her so much pain? Why did I not learn more from her? I should have been so nice to her not the jumped-up little renegade, fighting against her and everyone I met.

Thoughts unravelled in her mind, questioning who she was and how she had behaved. Turbulence and mania troubling her mentally. Indy had tried, she had been loving, special and mother like. She was pure.

Indy was her guardian angel and she had often treated her badly. Not allowing her to parent and guide fully. The internal struggle she had carried since birth did not allow Indy any real chance of helping her. Memories of her childhood floated to the top and created an uneasy feeling in her, rumbles and gurgles in her stomach made her feel unsettled as she saw for the first time how horrible she had been to be around.

With her head in her hands, the helmet hair draped over her fingers, which shielded her face from view, her feelings of confused hurt, anger and rage danced inside her demonically. A well-built onlooker once again was watching her, dressed in black with a black helmet still on and the dark visor closed. Dani had caught a glimpse of him through her matted hair and turned quickly to see nobody there. She was sure she had seen someone stood watching her.

"Excuse me miss you look like you have seen a ghost. Are you okay?"

A slender tall young man dressed in a suit, with an open neck shirt stood behind her and asked if he could join her, she did not reply. A blank face. An empty heart and a distrust glared towards him. He sat with her anyway, pulling a bottle of water from his jacket pocket. She slowly and silently stood up, as she turned to walk away his words struck her colder than she had ever felt, an ice-cold blade had ran up her spine and frozen her to the spot.

"I am a big fan of your dad, I saw you arrive on his death machine. When you left it at Ritchie's place, I knew it must be you"

The turn of pace she had would have out accelerated any bike, she stared back at him as if trying to turn him to stone, she clenched her fists and gave him a 1000-yard stare. The nervous chuckle noise he made raised her rage level more. With his hands up as if she had pointed a gun at him, his words froze her again. Explaining he was the journalist that covered her dad's story from the moment he took revenge on Dotty' killer, until he was murdered by the corruption of the law.

Rooted to the spot with a myriad of feelings sloshing around inside her, she looked far calmer that she felt, a mix of needing to run or fight erupted inside her. He passed her a phone with pictures of his news articles, the positive spin he had painted over the years mellowed her, as she tried to read the words, she muttered.

"Why have I never seen these?"

As she read them, she realised the stories Indy and Jack had told her were the same. the pictures showed how the articles painted her dad as a working-class hero, sticking it to the man. Only taking revenge on the evil in the world, many of the articles showed him as an innocent man protecting his family, avenging his family like a Viking would have.

A quizzical look appeared on her face as she gazed at the reporter.

"What do you want?"

He wanted to tell the final part of the story, how Dan's legend lives on, explaining how he wants to put Tania behind bars for killing her parents, he handed her a card with his number on it as she gave him the phone back. There were too many emotions exploding inside her to cope or make decisions.

"If I say yes, it's on my terms!"

Sat on her white and gold bike she still looked at him like he was the antichrist, showing him she was not to be controlled, she was free and he would never control her. Her words were simple and precise, and she pulled on her helmet. Her sleek cheek bones disappeared inside the white helmet.

"My world not yours!"

Unable to control her desire to showboat, she left with her front wheel slowly spinning freely in the air and the rear wheel firmly planted on the ground tearing at the black tarmac, the sun reflected off the brake discs and momentarily created a flash as she accelerated away. Emotions ravaged her, the thoughts of her mum and dad, the excitement that someone else wanted to see Tania pay and the fear of being tricked by him burbled through her mind louder than her twin exhausts.

Dani may have spent most of her time away from civilisation, but Jack had schooled her well in the way of the world. She was not aware in any way how similar Jack and Dan were, the fact that by learning her morals from Jack, meant she was in fact being taught much about the way her farther would have been.

Many miles of road were behind her and distance between the bike and the reporter grew. Was it wise? Was he honest? Could he help? The thoughts cascaded through until one thought stemmed them all. Where next?

A dirty B&B was her salvation for the night, her bike parked around the back of the old ornate building, painted in white with black eves.

Sitting on the bed with her old boots kicked off on the floor, she was able to relax a little, wondering what it would have been like working with her dad and learning from her mum. The desire for parental guidance ran strongly though her, the need for love and affection bellowed in her head.

She reminisced over the way Indy was, she thought deeply and the more she managed to block out the hatred for the world, the more she could see how lovely Indy had been to her. More importantly she could she how poorly she had actually treated Indy.

Memories flooded back into her mind as she remembered Indy sitting telling her stories of her wild adventures, especially the ones that happened after she met Dan. Indy spoke fondly the days riding the chopper and would often sit on it to tell the stories. The older Dani got the more her and Otto played with bikes, repairing them, modifying them and racing them, even before she could touch the ground on one. She had been given a wonderful childhood. Lots of love and security, she had been allowed fun and freedom. Her childhood was what many bikers would have loved.

The happiness floated around the room as she lay on the bed. She daydreamed about the time she nearly kissed Otto as a 13 year old. He was older than her and had pulled away as she tried to lay her lips on his. He was in his early 20's but she knew. The older they got the less that would matter. She only had to look at Indy and Jack to know that.

Warmth lay upon her, comforting her like a weighted blanket. Swirling her mid around with more happiness that she could ever imagine was possible. Drifting off into a deep sleep still wearing her clothes she had been in for days. She slept longer than she had ever slept before.

Woken to bird song, she saw the beauty of the room, she saw the small details, the pretty carvings in the wooden bed posts, the hearts on the wallpaper with detailed swirls in them. She also saw the crack in the ceiling, with mould embedded in the dirty line, she saw the discoloured net curtains and the aged wallpaper that had black stains around old ceramic ornaments. She was seeing the paradoxical views of the room. Life for her was as inconsistent as this, absurd and contradictory. The more she revelated on this the more she saw the opposing sides of Jack and Indy, she imagined the differences her mum and Dad would have had.

Yin and Yang was defiantly better as a whole. The two worked better together than apart, the two people supported each other, picked up the slack the other would leave and supported the strengths of the other. The world was beautiful but it was also dark, both needed to exist at the same time to balance each other. She had seen this her entire childhood modelled by Jack and Indy as she slowly allowed him into her world to complete her and each of them made the other a better stronger person. The stories they told of Dan and Joanne showed a couple who were an absolute powerhouse together. The bitter sweet songs of Dani's yesteryear sparked her mind, these invigorated her soul and gave her direction.

A strong will was now in place and the memories of the good she had, weighted against her bad, she knew the dark weighed heavy on her, the darkness was strong but the light was there too.

Stomping through the B&B she grabbed coffee and some pastries then headed for her bike. Sat upon it she felt complete. This bike truly was her style, the brightness of it contrasted against her darkness. The little bit of light radiating through her needed to be shared, needed to be directed to the right person.

The burner phone she had was not to be used freely, it still carried risk. This was important this light might go out any second. The phone rang only a couple of times, before a hurried voice came on with one simple word *Dani?*

"Indy I'm sorry, I fucked up. You didn't deserve how I treated you. You are perfect."

Indy was speechless and just as she opened her mouth old Dani was back, explaining how she could not be happy until she had avenged her Dad, how she had dealt with one of them on the list already. She rushed her last words to say, when the list was complete she would come home, until then she would tour the country righting the wrongs on the list.

Indy begged her to come home, but her words were not heard as she was left alone with the tone. The line was dead. Dani threw the phone on the floor and stamped the heel of her boot on the device.

"Game on"

No showboating as no one was there to watch, a calm and placid departure. She aimed the bike North. Yorkshire had been home for her dad and this is where it had to begin, no one had realised the stories they had told her as a child to comfort her, would turn her darkness to evil, redemption was coming for all those that had caused Dan pain.

CHAPTER 5: ORIGINS

Signs came and went, with Yorkshire now looming in front of her, a deep breath permeated it way through her. As she entered the homeland of her father. An uneasy feeling grumbled at her. Was she doing right? Was she on the side of good or was she on the side of evil? With these thoughts bouncing around her head, two names stomped into her mind and all the other questions fell away. These names were underlined and written in bold. These names were a big deal to her. What she was about to do, had to send a message. This had to be brutal. This had to look back to the origin of all this pain; this is the true beginning of what would Dan do?

The roads became leafier, with narrow roads sweeping left and right, a tight switch back which swung left up a hill tested her skills. Skilfully she powered up the hill, she was enjoying her bike more than ever and as she crested the knoll, an all too familiar lightness appeared at the front wheel. A grin opened up in her soul as the exhausts barked, now she was lost in the moment and looked ahead at the road, it was straight on, with the throttle wide open, she suddenly saw the road level off and turn right, she was travelling way too fast to make the turn. Thoughts swirled in her mind. Turn and hope the bike would make it or straight on? The decision was made for her as she ran out of road. She hit the brakes and entered a small car park at the entrance to a stately home. Stones flung up from the tyres and the front wheel squirmed under the load. What had happened? She was sure the road was straight on, this dusty little car park had saved her as a place of sanctuary, or she would have been in a field separated from her bike now. The annoyance in her mind burned. She hated making mistakes, a trait she was told was one of her dad's.

Thinking through the anguish she had over the two people she was searching for. Years of searching and planning all coming together in this very moment as she focused on the task in hand. Questions of morality plagued her, the influence of the Happy Hippy had more effect on her than she realised. The pendulum swung between what is right and what needs to be done, the metronome ticked inside her head.

Throwing a leg back over her bike, she caught a glimpse of that biker again all in black standing in the middle of the road, quickly she raised up her visor and she saw nobody. Thoughts of paranoia climbed into her mind. *Who could it be? Why do I see them? Why are they following me?*

Carefully riding passed the onlookers who had seen her recklessly ride into the car park, she did not care who they were, for she was searching for her emancipation. Her life of freedom. Her peace.

The exit from the road was no longer in her mind. Just the need to avenge her father's pain. A myriad of thoughts unravelled in her mind as she rode down the seafront, the smell of the fishing town assaulted her nostrils, screwing her nose up at the bitter smell. Buried deep in her memory the route from the seafront to the house of hate, she had done this route on a map more times than she could remember; Jack had also rode to this road with her as a pillion many times. It was where she had been destined to end up all of her life.

The bike coasted with the clutch pulled in, she rolled almost quietly along the little cul-de-sac. Jack had always been in two minds, every time he had been here, he left muttering, *"It's history we should let sleeping dogs lie"*. Dani had learned to be a good pillion from Jack, she had always adored growing up touring on the back of an old V-Twin. Skilfully she looped the bulbous turning area at the end of the road, she feathered the clutch, to pull up at number 23. Her bike idled momentarily outside the house before she turned it off and walked confidently down the drive as if it was her own property. A Scruffy old battered 4x4 with many parts removed, sat leaking oil on axle stands, whilst a slightly less scruffy 4x4 sat next to it. The smell of old vehicles and used engine oil was familiar to her, more familiar than her own father.

A white cheap plastic door with the letterbox flap missing stood in front of her, she tried the door handle and to her amazement it opened. Her mind electrified and her blood ran cold, all of her delicate hairs on her arms stood up, her breathing had intensified and she tried to control it, slow it down but her chest was tight and her eyes wide. The door was now opened slightly and she placed her leather booted foot through the door. Old shoes and boots lined the hall way and a smell of manure stung as it ricocheted along her nostrils. Her thoughts came, her mind bounced around like an excited child whilst her destiny controlled her. This was her truth, this was her life. This was her moment to stand up and be counted, fight for dad. She took a slow deep breath and stepped though the doorway her helmet still on and her visor closed.

As she closed the door, a frail woman's voice shouted down the stairs

"Is that you Margret? I will be down shortly"

Each step was slow and purposeful, all of her senses on overload, a cat ran out of a door to her left, darting across her path. Not even one step faltered as she appeared in the arched entrance to the room and stood dressed in full black leather, with a white helmet and black visor.

The man in the armchair sat up straight, with his eyes wide and his mouth equally wide open. He shook his head and wept, his tears slowly rolled down his heavily scarred face, years of healing could not repair the burns her dad had given him.

A leather gloved hand slowly opened the visor so she could stare eye to eye with the origin of all the problems in her life. She placed her finger towards her mouth under her helmet. His cries grew and his head shook from side to side faster as he mustered his words.

"No, no, no, no, no, not again"

Footsteps came running down stairs, followed by the repeated voice saying

"For fucks sake what's wrong with you now"

Dani stepped to the side hiding herself from view as an elderly ragged woman burst into the room and Dani stood with her jaw clenched and a small gun in her hand, with a silencer bigger than the gun its self.

Bang, one shot fired into her knee cap and the ragged woman fell to the ground clutching at her knee and screaming in pain. Bang second shot fired in to the other leg. Unshaken she stepped forward to the old man in the chair she almost whispered her words.

"Hear me. Fear me. Fear Dan! He tortured you for what you did. You continued the fight. It ends today"

Bang, shot three fired straight into his chest. His life ended there, the last chapter of his story came to an end as the red patch appeared in his grubby beige shirt, his tongue lolling to the side of his mouth as his head lay against the wing back chair.

"Now you fucked up you old bitch, you were not tortured. But you tried to kill my parents and you were there when they were murdered, you caused it, your demanded it, you begged for this moment, you summoned all this pain, you deserve to suffer"

Both her legs oozed a red mess all over the dirty heavily patterned smelly carpet. Dani walked closer to the now wailing mess of a woman on the floor, another whispered voice trickled from Dani's tongue.

"You nearly drowned my parents and then you stood back and watched them die, you caused this, he killed my grandmother whilst robbing her house, none of this is our fault. It's you, all you, ask yourself, go on ask yourself what would Dan do?"

Dani stepped back and removed her small rucksack, the zippers made no sound and the fresh oil on them glistened in the sunlight that flickered between the swaying trees outside the window, as the zip reflected the light it sent a dancing lightshow across the face of Dani, as she pulled out a tube, an orange funnel was attached to one end and it smelt of garage dirt, the orange funnel was scratched and battered with oil stuck in its grooves.

The colour drained from the yellow unhealthy face of the woman as Dani knelt down beside her, no words were spoken but the anger in her face silenced the old woman. Her memories plagued her, of the day she drove Dan off the bridge, forcing his bike into the river whilst Dan and Joanne were still on it.

Dani now had her knee pushed firmly into the woman's chest, no more fight was left in her as she lay bleeding to death. The filthy pipe was forced down her throat, the gag reflex just made Dani push harder, silent tears now soaked the old woman's face as the short pipe was lodged in her throat. The pain was excruciating with her eyes bulging red and the fear of what would happen next. Dani grabbed the bottle of water from her bag. She squeezed the water into the funnel as the once angry woman started to choke she spoke loudly and confidently.

"This is what my parents felt after you pushed them into the water. The burn in the lungs as the water entered them. Now drown bitch drown"

The choking noise engulfed the room and Dani placed her body weight on the old woman's chest as she now struggled to breathe, the woman's swollen eyes opened then closed rapidly and Dani yanked the funnel out of her throat. Rage filled her still. Pain kicked at Dani and evil ran in her blood. Calmly and precisely she stabbed the drowning woman in the side of the neck with a small blade, pulling upwards and outwards as hard as she could, puncturing the throat. The water and blood spurted out of her neck as the woman passed out, more red staining on the carpet from the top and the bottom of the fresh corpse.

With no haste and no urgency, Dani collected her now blood stained, oil filler funnel and packed them in a plastic bag loading them into her rucksack very calmly.

"From me to you, your work is started"

The words muttered as if a prayer to her deity. Casually Dani started her bike and allowed it to warm as she cleaned some of the blood from her leathers with some wet wipes.

As she opened the throttle her front wheel lifted and she was gone. A red patch had appeared on the pavement from the cleaning of her leathers. The pile of wet wipes stained with blood tossed on the front lawn, purposefully taunting the police, she knew Tania would be on the way, she knew Tania would be furious to be constantly one step behind just like she always had been.

The road welcomed her, separating her from her guilt as she enjoyed her only escape, the only moment she felt alive, really alive like she could be happy.

Stood looking at the mess in an old fashioned hovel of a house, two dead bodies now in body bags and the knowledge that there was no point looking at DNA to work out who was the murderer. Tania knew who it was, and she knew there would be no record of her anywhere. There would be no trace. It was Dan all over again.

Stomping out of the room her long coat flapped behind her like a cloak, she did not feel like a hero, she only felt anger and frustration. She needed to stop this cycle. Stop the wayward biker's path. With no regard for the scene she pushed passed the investigators and marched over the grass and kicked the red stained wet wipes in the air.

A fresh breeze swept over Dani's skin, the sweat and adrenaline had faded. Dani was now munching on fish and chips in an old backstreet sports bar. She hated it, drunken men shouting and arguing over which 1998 player had been the best in the world. She did not care, she was being low key, avoiding the biker hotspots and cafes that Tania would expect her to go to. The origins of the butterfly effect had been dealt with, she was revelling in the feeling, she was ecstatic to have avenged the death of Dotty for her family. The feeling swirled around her entire body, wishing she could have met Dotty and Morris, she had seen the pictures, and read the love letters that were in the garage back home, she wanted a romance like that, but who could love her when she could not even love herself? Sat in an old wooden chair with beer stained, faded red carpets, she dipped her last chip in her chilli sauce and left.

Everything had lost its taste; everything was in low definition and mono sound. She needed to taste again hear in stereo and see in high definition.

Nobody was there to congratulate her, tell her well done. It was time to do what she always did. Ride until she reaches her sanctuary.

Jack had always told her, in the real world, rather than the off grid utopia they had lived in as she grew up, she could have been a brain surgeon. She learned so fast in so much detail that she would have no problem learning any subject. She had studied all the routes Jack had taken her on, she had memorised all of the road numbers and now she headed for Block head, she had never liked calling him Brad, he had always been a fixer, a person that can set anything you want up. Block Head would find her a place to keep a low profile, while she searched for emancipation from her family's betrayal.

Block Head had set her up with a place of safety, she was now stood at a large old moss covered wooden door, the ornate hinges spiralled out to cover most of the old cracked surface. He tossed her the keys and rode away on his silent electric bike, he had tried to explain, for an incognito approach, electric was what she needed, Dani turned her head away and ignored the wise words which whispered in her ears, such a new-fangled way of powering the steel horse she enjoyed so much to ride. Air and fuel is king in my world she had thought. Behind her the sound of his tyres on the gravel drive crunched and fluttered into the distance, creating silence sooner than she expected.

The old heavy doors creaked open, she was easily able to ride her bike inside the large arched entrance. The old hospital had held over 150 patients at its peak. A place the most troubled people had been sent. A place where the world had tried to send the people it could not help; those people were lost, lost in a world of mental health and torture.

Pale blue paint flaked from the walls as she cautiously rode her bike down the high ceilinged corridor. The booming echo of her exhausts ricocheting around the walls and back down to her. For Dani this was a fantastic noise, a wonderful experience and a feeling of happiness, better than the philharmonic orchestra creating a crescendo.

Side stand kicked down and the keys in her pocket, she wandered into the first large room she saw. Rows of old beds lined both side of the room. Typical round tubular bed frames with dirty floral curtains hanging at the grubby windows. This was the place and the rucksack Block head had given her was full of the things she would need, a small butane stove, sleeping bag and everything else someone living off grid might need, he was almost as well planned as Jack.

The stories Jack had told of Dan always pleased her, she often tried to copy his ways and this was one of them for her. She sat eating a tinned curry and naan bread from the rucksack, the warmth from the little stove edged its way into her body. Stories of Dan and Jack competing to have the best laid out plan for every eventuality, had always left them laughing as she grew up, Otto told of how Dan would be grumpy when Jack had the upper hand or had spotted a weakness in Dan's plan. More often than not though, it was Dan who had the super plan. He was always the man with a plan.

Swigging on her whisky, the cold silver mouthpiece of her hip flask clinked against her lip piercing. Ideas of more body art excited her. Everyone she adored was covered in tattoos. She had only seen pictures of her parents ink. Indy's chest tattoo was to Dani the best tattoo she had ever seen. She had an idea in mind for her tattoo. It had to represent her, be her and show the world who she was.

Memories of years gone by flooded her thoughts, the stories that had shaped her being and the hatred she had for the modern world, Indy always said when Dani spoke of the world she heard Dan's voice.

The perils of moralistic decadence attacked her, the hatred of the corrupt in society trying to rob the poor of their freedom. These types were never satisfied without some pain and suffering along the way to riches. It was as insane as the people who had been held in the asylum she was now in. With nothing more than her bike and camping equipment. She felt tied up and trapped, trapped like a patient. Dani vowed to Indy many years ago, she would see evil go up in smoke, ruining the corrupt and stopping the financial debauchery of the world. Indy had always quoted her hippy lines of

"Two wrongs don't make a right" or *"an eye for an eye and we shall all soon be blind"*

Indy was far too pure to think like Dani.

Dani felt her personal revelations were the destiny of the corrupt, once they had made their money, it should cost them more. More than they think! It was thoughts like this that pushed her on, to avenge the common man and real people. She had been told many times to let it go before it drove her mad, the irony was not lost on her as she sat in the mad house tormenting herself with thoughts of the evil depravity, that some force on to the world, who consume it like a rock star with their first taste of cocaine.

The more whiskey she swallowed the more it consumed her, now drinking like a 'Navi' from the bottle in the rucksack. The sharpness of the peaty flavour was no longer catching her off guard, as she gulped down her escapism. She danced and sang at the top of her voice. 80s and 90s rock songs were her go to enjoyment. Her shrill drunken words slurring and echoing to the beat of her feet on the cold dirty tiled floor.

Drunken signing became drunken ranting. Screaming at those she despised, those on the list, those she need emancipation from.

A psychotic rage against the man, a social disfiguration of the truth, it was a distorted smile that hid the ugly truth of the minority, who had power and wealth. She was talking to herself, totally alone, separated from the social construct yet desperate now to be in amongst it. To change it and make the world a better place to be, a thought the one person could make a difference was a young person's thought, not that of person who has tried their entire life and failed to have the impact their young mind once craved. Change the moral compass of the world and leaving it spinning better. How many people could say they had achieved this? No matter how short this list was of people that had done this. She wanted her family name on it.

Dani had fooled herself into thinking she was alone in this mind set. Fighting for her place in the world. She had not had a father to tell her how it was going to be, so she fought alone. Her pain had aged her, created a hate in a young mind. It was now too late to take a step back, she didn't know what else she could do. Dani was lost in a myriad of pain, pain that was slowly consuming her young and innocent heart. No one she knew had been able to help her. She was now to find her own way, right or wrong, left in the cold dark asylum of her life.

Falling back on to the old hospital bed she spoke to herself, she reasoned with herself, the conversation became real, as if a person was there, a person talking to her, guiding her.

A voice, strong and deep sat her up straight, scared and now unsure if she was dreaming, drunk or mentally falling apart. Whose voice was it?

"Your path is your path, a correct path, make your choices and don't look back. You will walk proud in the cloud, in the halls of Valhalla. I made lots of mistakes on my own and I learned from them, my work was undone. Make it right"

The voice drifted away and she passed out, intoxicated with confusion and Bourbon.

Birds sang and the sun crept higher in the sky, a groggy feeling smothered her, consumed her, until the words from last night stomped through her mind. She wanted to join her Dad in Valhalla, but she was not ready to die, she had much she wanted to create in her life. The weight of her burdens felt heavy. The thoughts of what she was going to do, sat on her shoulders, a feeling of desire to right the wrongs and guilt intermingled with her. She had her Dad's anger on one shoulder and her mums reasoning on the other, with Indy's love of peace, gnawing at her thoughts as she set off on her way.

The routes were memorised and the list in her pocket, Dark Dani was back, dressed all in black, a faint stain darkened the leather around her cuff, the stain of what she had done. Riding slowly she contemplated her life, she contemplated who she was becoming, the feeling of confusion was back, the fear of continuing to disappoint Indy yet trying to become like her mum and dad.

Dani had always wanted to be like both Dan and Joanne, the perfect image of them, but first she wanted to wipe the slate clean. Her memory was as ever perfect, almost photographic. She found an old public phone and punched in the number, a number she had never rang before, a landline into Indy's room.

Indy cried immediately, she knew the only person who was not already in her house who knew this number was Dani. Tears almost made the words inaudible as she begged for Dani to come home.

Pleaded for her not to carry on with this list of revenge, explaining how they all could live here in peace and tranquillity, we need nothing else but what we have here.

Secretly a small tear plotted it way down Dani's cheek, a feeling she retained from a child, not one she had experienced as an adult until now. The words croaked through her new emotion.

"I know you are right but I have pain to off load before I can become the best type of person I can. A mix of you my mum and my dad. The pain is too much, it weighs me down, I must lose it. Once I am free I will return."

Indy cried more as she heard an angrier harder, nastier Dani. She feared she would never see Dani again. Fear that Dani will meet Odin in a blaze of glory. She had her dad's way. Never surrender. Never give up. Win or die trying.

The bike was once again righting her of her wrong doings, every mile she powered through, she left a little more guilt behind. Every time she watched the rev counter reach the red line, a sense of happiness danced in her mind. Every road was a symphony of delight as she approached the area she needed, the county she had wanted to visit most. Stories of her dad riding into the Derbyshire dales and heading for the biker haunts that were all over this county. The one she wanted most was on this road, a long road, a trade route of nearly 300 miles. As she sat in the café at the end of Snake pass she looked at the map, people sat on the table next to her describing the amazing twist and turns of the snake road, she had no time for tight turns and stories in her memories meant only the wide open trade route her dad had loved so much would do. Dani was literally about to join the infamous trade route and although she only had 37 miles of it to do. The next 20 minutes or so, were going to pay homage to the stories Jack had told, stories of races in the 1990s along the trade route to the best fish and chips in Derbyshire. There was a person she needed to meet. A person, who had hurt many people, financially and in many different emotional ways. A person her dad had read about and wanted to punish. A man on the list to avenge. The people this man damaged needed to be punished. This man was rumoured to be living high above the biking hot spot.

The hot black coffee slithered down her throat and the feeling it gave soothed her, coffee no longer made her hyper, it was a soothing relaxing stroke of ecstasy for her, only topped by the feeling whiskey gave her.

The coffee cup was now empty and the tank on her bike half full, she had the perfect recipe for escapism. The twin exhaust rumble as she started her bike pleased her, as she placed her helmet on, her mind sharpened; her darkness was creeping back into her calmness. There was only one way she knew how to silence her demons and that was a 3 figure assault on her senses.

Car after car was left in her wake, dust and debris from the centre of the road flicked up by her speeding rear tyre. Green and black was all she saw and she spliced her way through on a flash of white and gold, the bike was now part of her as she lay across the tank, with the vibrations of the bike reverberating through her breasts, sending shockwaves of pleasure through her nipples. Dani's senses were already high when she rode like this and non-more today as she mixed the pleasure of her machine with the excitement of writing the balance of wrongs. Carving her way through the Derbyshire rock faces, leaning her bike closer to the tarmac, her toe grazed the ground and the feeling excited her more. Gently opening the throttle, she powered on faster and faster until it happened. She stuck out her knee and the elation rumbled through her as she gently allowed her knee to follow the bumpy surface. The left hand bend straightened and immediately dropped in to a right. Again the feeling delighted her as the rough surface scuffed her knee slider. Dani was in a seventh heaven. Dani was removed from the world and all her darkness forgotten. A smile so big was covering her face, hidden by her white helmet and black visor. She was incognito to the world and she loved it.

As she approached the last couple of miles the queuing cars did not hold her up, downshifting, her revs climbed, with each gear change and her smile was even more exaggerated, her eyes wide and her heart raced. Almost the entire part of this last few miles she attacked whilst over the central white line, with the cars stationary waiting to move forward and the vehicles on her right allowing her to power between them. The racing heart beat slowed as she took a deep breath. Hundreds of motorbikes lined the road on the right and then it appeared a space outside the chip shop and the river flowing to her left. Happiness filled her spirit and the bike filled the space.

With the engine now off her mind slowed and he happiness filled her. The smell engulfed her nostrils as she took her helmet off, the sharpness of the salt and vinegar hit her hard followed by the fatty smell of deep fried fish and chips. She had never had the fish and chips that Jack and Indy often reminisced about. Her helmet was now neatly placed on her mirror, she was in and out the shop like a flash, sat at the chrome table with her food warming her hands, she placed a hot chip in her mouth and the feeling nearly knocked her backwards, they were nothing like the French fries she was used to, these were fat and chunky, the salt made her mouth dance, she ripped of a piece of the battered fish and was bowled over by the sensation. The next several minutes she saw nothing around her, just the pure pleasure of stuffing her face on traditional fish and chips in a biker filled quaint village.

The sun warmed her face and the hot food warmed her soul. A full belly and an ice cold traditional fizzy drink teased it way to her delight, apparently one of her dad's favourites, dandelion and burdock. It was a taste sensation which gave her a satisfied feeling like she had never experienced before. Gazing at her bike parked next to a black Bobber, the contrast was startling and she liked it.

The moments of bliss had come in revelations; however she had work to do. She had a score to settle. A deep breath was no match for the weight of that feeling that tempered her happiness. A soft happy voice appeared in her ear.

"Nice bike that, mine is the Bobber next to yours"

The aging biker sat in his brown leather jacket, sipping a cold drink as he ate his last few chips. He waffled on about the heritage of these bikes the twins and triples, the way the style was timeless. The old man reminded her of a softer Jack. She respected the old school bikers and even though she was now starting to fill with the rage of revenge. She kept her composure and made her excuses to leave. The biker nodded with a small smile placed on his face, he sat watching the world go by, with clearly no place to be and nowhere to rush off to. She envied him, she wanted to feel like that. But first, where was the monster? The monster who had taken from the common man.

Dani backed her bike out of its parking space, the cars here were used to driving around manoeuvring bikes in the road, she started the bike and the old biker raised his steaming coffee and gave her a wink. It felt like home. The old biker felt like, well she had no idea but it felt good.

Sat on her bike the vibrations calmed her, but rage was there bubbling inside her as she contemplated what she was about to do. The man resting in her mind was a thief, who had stolen from a successful businessmen, collapsed multiple profitable companies for his own gain and worse, he had stolen from peoples savings, stolen pension money, he had robbed from the rich and the poor and kept it all for himself.

A check over her shoulder and the road was clear enough, lots of throttle and a small wheelie as she sped off past the hordes of bikers wandering around the quaint village. It was a place of happiness and a place where all people are equal, rocker, hippy or eccentric anyone was welcome.

A hard right that doubled back on its self, stretched up into the hillside, the fence to the right had seen better days and the top rail had been broken off, hanging down over the second fence rail. As her bike exhaust noise rose, so did the bike. Slowly making its way up the steep incline, climbing higher and higher. The view to her side appeared, she could see the hordes of bikers wandering and the few sat outside the chip shop. She paused and gazed down over the area, the river cut its way through the rock face and the road ran alongside it, the houses behind her would be her perfect location. A place to watch the masses, but not have to be close to them, until she chooses. Dani had to limit her time with large groups, she became exhausted by them. Growing up she had lived with only a few people around her and only small villages surrounding them. This biker haven was beautiful, but far too busy for her to stay too long.

The houses had been small and like workers cottages, quaint and modest. Slowly she looked further along the small road and there it was, many times she had seen this building in photographs; a grand building imposed itself into the road, edged with large white cornerstones. This was a house of grandeur, a house of money, a house of pain to come.

Riding her bike straight onto the small piece of land to its side, she sat there in her white helmet and blacked out visor, tight black leathers whilst sitting on her white bike. The pain of all the people, damaged by greed from the owner of this house was growing inside her. She looked over the road below, waiting for the circus to begin. The door at the front flew open and an angry voice appeared.

"You can't park there! Get your bike down there with the rest of them. This is private...can't you read? No access it said!"

Her head turned and the dark visor hid her anger, as she got off the bike the voice became angrier still, telling her to get of his land, demanding to know who she thought she was.

She stepped towards him, he was a tall man not muscular and not thin, with floppy hair and checked summer shirt flapping in the breeze. Dani didn't hesitate; she leant forward and marched at him. The shock silenced him and rooted him to the spot. As she unzipped her jacket she pulled out a small machete. His face appeared to widen as horror took control of him. A small circle of wee grew in his crotch as he ran back in to the house. Dani was young and fast, already at the door as he turned to close it. She shouldered the door with her tiny frame which hit him in the face knocking him unconscious.

A crashing boot stomped over the lavish threshold, she closed the door behind her and locked it. The room was more ornate that she could ever imagine.

Slowly she took off her helmet and placed it on the table in the hall.

"Well Mr Wolf I have come to blow your house down"

CHAPTER 6: RUNNING WILD

Dazed and confused the floppy haired man lifted his head, immediately feeling the pain in his forehead, a small cut on his eyebrow showed where the door had hit him. The leather clad attacker now stood tall over him, this created a bewildered fear, questioning why?

His words were stuttered and rushed as he tried to make sense of what had happened. Questions of who and why blurted out, statements of *'Take what you want it's all rented anyway',* were thrown around in a spineless flurry of fear to try and save himself.

"You don't need to know who, only why!"

Dani explained how he had ended up on her list, confusion was strewn across his face as he could not understand why someone would care what he had done, if it was not directly affecting them.

Her disgust for his poor morals was nothing in comparison to her disgust for his lack of fight and his weakness. Dani preyed on weak men like this who acted the big man in public.

"You have a debt to pay and that debt is due with interest!"

The fear had now turned into laughter, he shook his head and his laughing became louder as he stood up holding his bleeding head. His words trickled along the floor to the distaste of Dani.

"The government have seized all my money, tax office, pension office and the fuckin' bank, everything I have is begged borrowed or stolen".

A deep intake of breath appeared to echo across the room, a strong female voice struck fear into the crude, rude and gregarious man, stood now expecting forgiveness.

"I am not here for your money, I am here to avenge the downtrodden common man, I am here for your life"

An expression of horror rolled around his face and fear caused his tremble. He reached for a hunting knife that was hanging on the wall. With his arm outstretched he stepped towards the knife, his legs created a v shape. Dani slid along the polished floor both feet first, thrusting her small knife upwards as she slid beneath him, the blade pierced his testicles through his linen trousers, ripping his scrotum wide open.

High up on the hillside no one could hear him scream, no one would want to come to his aid even if they did hear him. He had robbed many bikers over the years and cheated more people than he could remember.

Clutching his bleeding crotch he writhed on the floor. The small frame of Dani stood over him once again, with his hunting knife glinting in the sun lay on the floor, the bright light peaked through the blinds as she now slowly played with his knife above him.

Tears ran as fast as his blood. His hands held his balls in place, one of them already poking out of the wound.

"You had balls of steel to do what you did, pity they are not really that strong"

Dani brought the knife straight down through his hands, the expensive knife sharpened for use on wild game sliced easily through his flesh. A squelch took centre stage in the room as the bowie knife, passed through the hand and into his gonads. The cold sharp steel sliced everything it touched with ease.

Slumped on the floor was a business titan, a draconian master, a devil in plaid. Now lay with blood pouring from his loin and his face turning grey. He had passed out from the pain, now helpless and dying fast.

The base of the hill was a happy space filled with bikers enjoying their machines, drinking their beverage of choice, munching on fish and chips. At the top was an evil man who they all hated, unbeknown to them he lay with his once steel balls now hanging between his legs, the skin ripped open and the testicles exposed. Dani rolled him over and over through the large ornate door, until he was lay on the edge looking down the hill, she stared down on the merriment. She took one last look at the vista, with the river, rock face and road snaking all as one with the happy people all going about their normal sunny Sunday. The bleeding business tycoon now barely alive as his life seeps away into the grass; his eyes flickered as his gained a faint consciousness. She placed her boot on his back and rolled him down the hill.

Screams and shouting rumbled up the hillside as she put her helmet back on. Her thoughts turn to her list, she pulled out the crumpled aging note and ticked off the next big one she had on the avengement order. A sadistic smile rippled into the corners of her mouth. The triple wail from her exhaust drowned out the noise and she disappeared. The pandemonium was taking place below her.

Cautiously she rode down a very steep descent, there was gravel on the floor at the junction, which created a nervous feeling. Bikers now rushed over to the base of the hill to try and catch a glimpse of the screaming man who lay bleeding to death. A few young bikers had already made it on foot to the now gasping for air man, with an amateur orchidectomy laid out in front of them. The femoral artery in his groin was now pumping blood through its roughly torn gash between his legs.

One of the young men took off his own tee-shirt, revealing a well-defined torso. As he knelt down to try and apply pressure to the wound. A final gasp of air was exhaled and the wounded man went quiet. The have a go hero slumped into the sticky red stained grass.

"We are too late bro, who the fuck do-ya think he upset?"

No answer came as his pal vomited his fish and chips back up, burning on the way out as his last meal splashed on to the grass, mixing with the dark red end of a life.

Pandemonium created a frenzy of people all clambering on bikes to ride up to see if they could help, just as Dani coasted over the gravel in the junction she slowly slipped away. No peacocking, no showboating, no drama.

A large group of bikes all sat on their stands next to the old weak fence, overlooking the jewel of the Peak District, nobody noticed Dani exiting along the road, heading North, nor did they notice the biker dressed in black, still wearing his helmet stood on the opposite side of the river, leaning on the railings with the meandering river, babbling in front of him. He watched Dani leaving, his black helmet nodding slowly as she left.

The bikers at the top of the hill all focused on the brutal murder of a man. Gathering around, not one picture taken, just a few calling the police. With a slow chant burbling over the mayhem, an old man sat on his even older bike, singing the words to the last post, while intermittently mimicking the sound of the bugle. The haunting notes rippled through the hill side. A loud voice shouted over them, almost drowning the sombre notes with an angry voice.

"Isn't that the guy who ripped off his workers in his factory? Owes loads of bikers money too"

The following noise overshadowed the moment, stamping over the sincere sorrow people felt, replacing it with a macabre glee. With comments of 'Well he's got his comeuppance now'. It wasn't many minutes before the sirens silenced all of them and the group of 50 plus bikers fled leaving a handful of people who wanted to do the right thing stood around the dead man, with nothing covering his dignity but the breeze.

Tyre noise now echoed its way around them as the police cars now loomed into view, the incline caused the tyres to spin on the loose surface announcing the arrival ceremonially. Tania barged past them all as the uniformed police and started to take notes of people's names. Tania's voice screeched over them with the more nastiness than anyone of the crowd had heard before.

"Get these stupid bikers off my crime scene. Fukin' dicks! They are ruining any shred of a lead"

Enraged by the outburst one biker climbed back over the fence, started his blue and white bike then left in rolling burnout of stones and debris, which flicked up at Tania and the remaining bystanders. Times had changed, Tania was weary, worn down by the biker scene she had become immersed in it for all those years hunting Indy and Dani. She could no longer be bothered with one hot headed dick on a sports bike, she had met every type of biker you could imagine, watched every internet video on the types of bikers you might meet, and she despised them all, but none more so than she did Dani. Dan's daughter had taunted her, as if Dan was still alive, she felt an odd feeling every time she arrived at a scene caused by Dani, but she could not work out why.

The ride back to the old mental asylum was feral, Dani barely shutoff the throttle, her tortured tyres spat little balls of rubber from the edge of the tyre as she cornered. Dani was now riding like her dad had, wild and reckless, two peas in a pod. She was now running wild, escaping from the world, evading Tania and dodging her pain. No matter what she did her pain rode pillion with her, she merely forgot about it the faster she rode. The pain never left her; it clung on as if it was part of her.

The rusty old gates groaned as she pushed them open, she wheeled her bike into the dusty entrance and rode it straight in to the old asylum, the corridors were long and high, the paint peeled and the dirty curtains flapped behind her as her bike wailed its way up and down the wide corridors, the tyres squealed a high pitched pain as she tormented them, just as her memories agonized her.

One solo figure appeared in front of her, the huge frame of a man felt like it filled the large corridor. It was Blockhead, he had been waiting for her, he told her, that what she had done in Derbyshire was hard to hide, even Dan could not hide from Tania forever. He explained that Jack was now demanding to know where she was.

"He wants you back in Harz."

The silence from Dani was all the answer he needed, he knew how much she was raging in her helmet right now.

"I can hide you 'til the morning, then I will have to tell Jack where you are."

She asked him to stay, for no other reason but to make sure he doesn't tell Jack until she had left. She planned for the first time in her life, not to follow

Jack's wise orders. This had become an obsession. She would finish the list, no matter who tried to stop her.

The cold night air meandered around her, brushed against her face and kissed against her lips. The fresh air kept her awake and her revelations came thick and fast. The thoughts kicked at her and pained her. The only thought that rose above the pain, brought its own pain. 'The only way to have happiness and freedom is to chase it, it won't come to you' Dani was creating her happiness, Dani was avenging her pain, in the hope she could escape with nothing but the happy hippy mind set, which Indy had tried to instil in her. She missed Indy so much and wanted to make her proud. But first she needed to make her Dad proud.

The sleep depriving spiral of thoughts ran at her and danced through her soul. *'Am I making my dad proud? Is finishing his tormented pain, what he would want? What would he do now if he were me?'*

As the sun peeked through the broken window and brought her back from a half sleeping state. She looked over at Blockhead who still had a bottle of whiskey in his hand as he slept. Quietly she slipped into her leathers. Laced up her chunky boots and wandered over to her bike. The engine burbled into life and Blockhead opened his eyes, she turned to look at him, though her dark visor. The contrast of the white helmet was over exposed by the early morning sunshine bouncing of the white, gold and black details. A small salute was given from her brow, as she turned away. Moments later and she was gone into the brightness of the day.

An awkward smile teased its way across Blockhead's face. He picked up his phone and dialled the only number on that contact list. His voice was precise and low.

"I saw Dani, she was in Yorkshire, she is safe for now, but you need to extract her fast. That bitch Tania is literally gunning for her like she did Dan!"

The only words that came back were '*Thank you brother*' before the phone went silent again.

Indy rested her hand on Jack's shoulder, the love they had created over many years was strong, the bond was unbreakable.

"Bring her home Jack, save her please"

A tear appeared in Indy's eye and Jack bushed it away as he looked at her with zero emotion in his face. A stoic glare hit her. It had been many years since she had seen that look upon his face staring at her. She had become more accustomed to the love he showed her, the care and affection he gave her every day. This is what had made her very happy.

Jack's lips were tight and his fear for Dani repressed. He pulled on his dirty old boots, his gravel noted voice crashed from his mouth.

"I will fetch Dani myself and I will end Tania"

He leaned forward, put both his hands on Indy's waist and pulled her in close. His kiss was tender yet cold. Indy knew this Jack. This was an old Jack. This was the Jack from 20 years ago. He looked her deep in the eyes. A look so deep she could feel it. He silently mouthed the words *'I love you'* and with that he was gone, in a cloud of blue smoke from his aging bike.

Indy crashed down in her comfy wing back chair and wept. A mix of feelings came as she feared the outcome for Dani and Jack. She mused over the happiness Jack had brought to her. Never did she ever imagine how happy Jack would have made her. She drifted into a catatonic state, pushing away her fear and anxiety, replacing it with happy memories of Jack.

The thoughts tumbled and twisted, bringing with it the happiness she had shared with Jack. Eyes closed tightly and a large smile now drifted across her face. The happy life tiptoed through her feelings. Never had she felt so bright, as when she visualised Jack stood in front of her the first time she saw him. His old yet young appearance struck her, her memory of how all women looked at him, the memory of how he looked at her. A steely look but a cheeky glint burst through as their eyes connected. The grey fleck in his long hair and his salt and pepper beard had melted her. The 'dad bod' he had, only completed the look and made her fancy him more. He was then just starting to show is age yet retain his youth. She had wanted him from the start. The truth was she had wanted anyone who made her feel safe. She had a penchant for the strong older man, who could get stuff done. Dan had complicated that for her. In her dizzy young mind she could not figure out what she wanted. Reality was in those days she was young and naïve, thinking that 'free love' and a hippy approach to monogamy would work.

As the years aged her and her maturity grew. She realised she wanted the security of growing old with one person. A person who was her equal. A person who wanted to lover her as much as she loved them. Jack showed her that love and treated her like a princess but never acted like a king. This is exactly why he became her king and her love for him grew.

The man in faded black clothes had danced in to her heart. It was just them two in the world when he was next to her. 20 years ago, every man wanted to be Jack and every woman wanted to be with him. The more Indy had pushed him away the more he was intrigued by her. No woman had ever made him chase her, he had never yearned for a woman. They had all been so easy for him. Indy had been very different. She had made him want her, made him chase her, made him feel like he could not have her.

Indy felt like the last hour had been days, she felt as if the world was taking her happiness away, taking her love away, taking her world away from her. Daydreams of laughter came with the memories of years gone by. Jack and Indy had spent many hours sat out on the veranda, drinking and laughing often until the sun came up. They had seen many sunsets and sunrises come and go without sleep in between. They had made love frequently with the fading warmth caressing their naked bodies as the sky turned to a wonderful display of shimmering red's and yellow's with a flourish of pink's.

Her hand wandered down her neck, as she daydreamed of Jack's embrace, the roughness of his hands and the softness of his touch. The way he made her feel as his breath trickled past her ear lobe, he would whisper how he adored her. How he loved her and how much he wanted to get his beard wet with his head between her thighs. Memories of giggling as he spoke to her and how she told him she loved the change of romance to filth. She had always referred to his filthy talk as his garage talk, the kind of smutty jokes he would tell with his mates in the garage he once owned.

The sun now faded on her sat alone, she wished so much that it was Jack stroking her neck and caressing her nipples. He knew how sensitive they were to Indy and had always kissed and tickled them with his bearded mouth. Indy drew her legs up high on the sofa, she was relaxed on the veranda, dreaming of Jack now kissing his way down her chest, gently playing with one nipple between his fingers and kissing his way across her stomach, with the other hand gently moving its way up her inner thigh. Indy was yearning for Jack to be there, she already wished, she had his engorged cock in her mouth. She loved to suck it and drive him wild. But for now she gently rubbed her clitoris and one of her nipples as she imagined Jack now with his beard soaking wet between her legs. As his tongue danced in and out, up and down, pleasing and teasing her to the very edge of orgasm. Her imagination was now in full flight, viewing previous times with Jack. Her skin was pricked and all the hairs in her arms stood up. Her head arched backwards and she started to moan with delight. Her voyeuristic view of Jack now knelt on the settee next her. His large fingers deep inside her, bouncing off of her G spot as he pressed down on it from her stomach with his other hand and his tongue still flicking across her clitoris. She would always slowly be teasing his hard cock as he made her teeter on the edge of orgasm. She was always ready to take his cock deep in her mouth and suck him hard until he exploded over her tongue with a salty delight. Indy screamed an almighty orgasmic crescendo to her fantastic fantasy fucking.

The sun was now low in the sky, barley illuminating the rolling hillside in front of her, the exposed skin almost itched, as she shuddered as the last of her orgasm rippled over her. The ecstasy of her solo fun still making her quiver and retain a happy memory of Jack. Slowly the enjoyment faded as she pulled a Sherpa fleece blanket up over her electrified skin. The warmth in the air was fading, the happiness she had tumbled as she hoped that she had not lost Jack forever. She feared Jack may never actually return. She feared Tania would kill him and Dani just like she had vowed after killing Dan.

Jack rode his bike with very little haste. He had many thoughts running through his mind. He knew he had to rescue Dani.

He was furious that she had disrupted his perfect life in the Harz Mountains, chasing ghosts that did not need to be chased, Jack had aged and now was happy with his peace. He did not want any drama or grief. He was watching his happiness in slow motion drifting away. Jack was anticipating the worst, yet he never hesitated, he so desperately wanted to turn and return to his happiness, he wanted to hear Indy call his name or utter the words he loved to hear. A wry smile and a pained squint came across him as he heard the words in his head *'keep talking, I am nearly there'* Indy drove him wild with those words, those words always ended up with his beard getting very wet. Nothing however would ever match the words he heard daily, the words that took him to a secret place in his heart, as he watched her in slow motion say *'I love you'*. No matter how wild he was running in life, those words melted him and made him always want to get home to Indy. He had never loved anyone before and Indy had all the love he had never been given. He gave it all and never wanted to be apart from her for longer than a tank of fuel would last.

With a straight dirt road ahead of him, he could see a chain link fence. It had been many years since he rode along this road. He knew grief and drama was about to savage him. He turned off his bike and sat motionless as the dusty dirt road settled around him, the sun glinted off his mirrored aviator sunglasses and the reflection in them started to change. The gate opened and an Enok drove out of the gate at speed. It had been a lifetime ago since Jack had been in one of those vehicles and it had not always been for the right reasons. The German military police were not people that played at the job. They took it very seriously. The Enok pulled up alongside him and two soldiers got out, one holding a Heckler and one a Koch G3. Jack did not move a muscle, he knew this equipment well and was very aware a wrong move now would trigger panic in these two young military police officers. They spoke in German and asked him to state his business or leave.

Jack still did not move, nor did he turn his head and look at them. He simply and calmly spoke in German to the two officers.

"I am Old Red, I wish to see the Triple Striped flag"

The Two officers stepped back, one of them quoted the phrase into the radio, the reaction crackled back 'Scheiße, ich dachte, er wäre tot'.

The two officers looked surprised, when the order was given to escort him to the Major's office.

Jack thumped along the wooden floor in his trademark paratrooper boots, his green combat trousers were tucked inside them and the collar of his military shirt protruded from the slightly undone zip of his aged black leather jacket. The Major stood to attention and saluted, Jack returned the mark of respect. As they shook hands the grip was strong from both, the tone of the voices softened and the two young soldiers were excused. Jack stood silently with a stern look on his face and as a mark of respect to his German brethren, he would only speak in German. He had served alongside this man in Afghanistan. They had both risen up the ranks together and been in charge of allied regiments. The two old soldiers momentarily stood silent. The German major broke the silence.

"Jack it's been a long time, if you are stood on military ground again, the shit must really have hit the fan in your life. My regiment and I, owe you our lives, you are still seen as a hero, the stories of you in Afgan are still told about you regularly. Those young soldiers will want to shake your hand if I tell them who you are"

The old biker stood there and nodded as he looked him straight in the eye. He explained how he only ever did his duty and was proud to have served alongside him. Jack placed a bag on the floor in front of him, the German Major stepped back from it.

"If that is a bag of money, your money is not welcome here. You however can have my help in any way you need. What do you need brother?"

Jack swallowed hard and stifled his emotion he wanted to pay his way so often, he would not insult people by forcing cash upon them if they said no, he also would not insult them by not offering to pay his way. Jack had many stories of bravery that he had never told anyone, not even Indy. Many people owed their life to his heroism and his tactical ability to extract people from warzones. He had taken several bullets in his military career, when all else failed he would go in alone to rescue people. The last time he did this he had dragged the German Major away from a firing squad. Who were just loading ammunition ready for an execution. This is why Jack's shoulder always hurt so much. He had torn the ligaments in his own shoulder, dragging him into an Enok before driving him back to the base. Not once did he ever mention the bullet he took to the buttock. Only the medical team knew about that one. He had been told it would be a kamikaze mission to rescue the Major on his own. The order had been to leave him there to face the firing squad. Jack even in the military had played by his own rules.

With the pleasantries now exchanged Jack and his bike were loaded in to a U.K. M. The German Major explained, that this is on loan to us from the U.K. we have an exchange to do; the crew is English and will fly with us. Jack smiled and patted his old friend on the back with a firm slap. Jack swallowed hard and did not look at the Major as he uttered the words.

"Thank you Karl"

The old Chinook's rotors started and the whining noise from the motors intensified as they straightened out the blades. Jack took a deep breath; the anguish of war still pained him. This was no nostalgic feeling as the whines turned into the familiar twin rotor blade slap between the two vortex's. The slap and snap was now at full speed and the feeling of a soft accent into the air came. Jack's mind rumbled on, as the blades beat to the distinctive rhythm of the 200 MPH monster. There was now no return. Jack's mind was in full military flight too. He was once again a soldier who will do whatever it takes to complete the mission. Extract Dani, kill Tania return the subject alive to Germany. Jack was now his old, bold and cold military self again.

The journey was smooth and fast cruising at just under 200 MPH, Jack looked at his bike strapped down near the loading end and even that did not bring any emotion or feeling. He was in full weapon mode and his war face was back, Karl gave Jack a sideways glance and saw the 1000 yard stare, the look of a man who could commit any kind of atrocity and still march on to skull fuck a man, who had crossed him. Karl knew Jack was the most dangerous man he had ever met. His bravery and single track mind made him see in shades of green only. His bravery made him able to achieve more than any other solider Karl had witnessed in his long and distinguished career.

Karl feared this mission was different, this was personal and this could get very messy very quickly. This could be very hard to hide from the media. This could be hard to explain and end his career in the military. Karl shook his head and chuckled, honouring his debt to Jack was more important than anything else. He questioned Jack on the protocol of this mission. The words were stern, the words were precise, but his eyes did not leave the fixed position he had.

"Find Dani protect her at all costs, load her and the bike and leave Tania bleeding to death, while I watch her take her last breath, the last face she sees will be mine!"

CHAPTER 7: INCOGNITO TO THE WORLD

Aimlessly riding through tree covered roads; a realisation hit her that life was a game, nothing more nothing less. The rules of life were hard and Dani did not recognise them as her game! Revelations now smashed through her world and unsettled her.

She did not want to let life pass before her eyes as many people did, aimlessly drifting from nowhere to somewhere. That kind of lifestyle cost life in Dani's eyes. Plans are denied without actions. She started to sing in her helmet as she rode, an old song Jack had played many times flickered through her. Her thoughts settled into a vicious turmoil as she took a deep breath and tried to silence her evil.

Words tumbled through her mind, she would have loved to have stayed in Harz. She hoped if she never returned they would think fondly of her. She had said goodbye to them all many times in her own head, preparing for the day she hoped would never come.

Goodbye should have been the last words they ever heard of hers. She never actually said it to anyone at all. She never hugged Indy and apologised for being such a bitch. She regretted the way she had left home, the way she had treated people and that she had never loved anyone truly.

Pain was sticking pins in her brain. It literally hurt inside her head. Her mind used her words against her. Telling her if she had a heart it would be breaking now. Leaving had been easy, what she carried with her was not.

Hurriedly she pulled her bike to the side of the road and knelt in the grass with her helmet tossed beside her. Atrocities beat her insides as she knelt on all fours. Eyes closed red pain seared around them and hot pokers jabbed into her brain as she ran cold. Sickness and pain controlled her mind as it wailed, broken and in need of help.

Darkness tapped her on the shoulder, a whisper flowed into her soul. This is it, this is where you say goodbye to the world. Your time has come. You are at the end of your road.

Dani argued with her inner monologue, she had not seen enough of life, she had been cheated of a childhood and needed to right her wrongs, then do good in the world before she rested.

Then it happened, tears came and the relief was huge. Some of her pain was leaking down her face and dancing down the blades of grass beneath her. Each tear made its decent to the floor, shedding some of the problems in her mind as if a snake was shedding a layer of skin.

Dani sat next to her bike and shook her head and rubbed her temples, begging for the pain to go, with the black mess still prodding her inside her head, telling her it was time. Thumping and droning. The inner voice overpowered her and tired her out. She looked through the green and orange autumnal tree canopy and she saw a twin rotor helicopter approaching, the noise was intense as it passed overhead. She imagined the blades cutting her into pieces and ending it all for her. Old music flooded into her mid and lyrics from a bygone era started to bite at her. Revelations came more and more:

'Why do I give a fuck? I have reached the end but others need to be ended! Don't care if I end myself ending others! Take my chances fixing the world! I am nearly dead anyway! I wish someone was there for me, rather than myself. I am empty, cold, spiralling in chaos and creating darkness'

Her final thought broke through to her, smashing its way to the front. This all started with Tania and it has to end with Tania. If that does not kill my pain, my world has to end right there.

Dani had wanted love on a higher level, but the questions and pain is all she had, no mother, no father just a sickness growling inside. This was her final flight. She needed to be ready; she needed to be right in her own mind when she found Tania. Not the mess that she was. This was it. All Dani wanted was to be, out of sight, out of mind, out of everything. Her last chance to shed the pain and disappear in happiness was blowing in the wind once again. She could not go on living this way!

Dani slowly threw her long slender leather clad leg over the bike, the seat hugged her and the bars pulled her in close. In her life this was the closest she could feel to a parental hug. The feeling of safety started to creep back in as she searched for the thing that brought her the most pleasure, a flowing ride into the countryside looking for a place to call home for the night. A place to quench her thirst and cleanse her soul is what she needed. She needed some time to repair her broken mind, before it was too late.

A collection of tables with a small collection of bikes sat glistening in the evening sun. A bike night was just what she needed. Sitting with a brew she started to look at the bikes and watch the bikers arriving. It's a rough old roadhouse style place, with a greasy food van outside the pub its self, with signs for camping and rooms for the night. An interesting guy was collecting glasses; his hair was tied back in a ponytail. He looked like every American image of an aging biker. Dani felt at ease as soon as she saw him. She had seen so many photographs from Indy and Jack of people that looked just like this bar owner. As soon as she took her helmet off he smiled at her, but barley looked at her. He was not your pervy old man just a genuine guy. As soon as he spoke it was even more obvious he was just a regular old guy who loved his biker pub. His local dialect warmed her, he spoke with some odd phrases the words he said sparked a memory as she wandered towards the food van 'A up me duck'. She had heard this said before, Jack had joked about his time in parts of the Midlands, where duck was a term of endearment, used by all the locals to great delight to visitors.

She placed her helmet on the wall next to the van and ordered a greasy burger with a cup of tea. A warm haze raced from the cup, the smell of the meat tantalised her and hunger shouted at her. She stood eating her food, the smell in the air had enticed her, drew her in with a promise of happiness, the warmth flowed inside her as the guilty pleasure drifted through her. As she ate, more and more bikers came and went, the night was in full flow and the old road house was packed. One old biker was saying to his mate 'I have been coming here since the early nineties and this place hasn't changed one bit and that's what I like best about it'.

The cooling brew warmed her hands as she took in all the sights around her. Old classic bikes, new pocket rockets, small and big, plus the odd back patch milling around. She loved being incognito to all but part of the frivolity. It suited her well taking in the sights and smells but under no pressure to converse with anyone unless she chose to.

The owner was still working the greasy food van, a red haze clung in the sky as the sun started to set, the crowd started to disperse. He wandered around like the king of his manner, tidying up and smiling to himself. Dani's thoughts turned to Indy. It was similar to a place she had described, although she had refused to tell the entire story of everything that went on that night.

"A up me duck, do you do rooms for the night here?"

She chuckled inside after trying the local dialect, she knew it did not suit her accent, which was an odd mix of English and German. The owner smiled at her sweetly, hardly making eye contact, explaining that they have many bunk beds that many people have slept in.

'Although you don't want one of those, I will get my wife to make you a fresh bed up in one of the solo rooms'.

As he wandered past the outside tables he shouted his wife and asked her to make up a bed. He then disappeared in to the pub. Dani felt like she belonged for the first time, the black and white signs above the door had a picture of Queen Victoria on and the windows were full of adverts for live music. It was not the Ritz, but that's what made it perfect.

Just as she started to gather her things from her bike the owner shouted

'Don't be leaving that pretty bike outside, I will open the garage'.

A Thursday bike night had finished and only the bar staff were left. They all laughed and joked as they cleaned up the bar area, the atmosphere was already good, just from the staff alone, She imagined what it would be like listening to some heavy metal or new style county singer. A sign next to her showed the names of the upcoming acts and it was a mix of old rock with the one Derbyshire girl who had clearly made it in the world of Country playing next week. Dani felt like she could stay a while, she knew Jack and Indy would love it here. She felt that her mum and dad would have been the kind of people to frequent such a place too.

She needed some fun, she needed some rest and most of all she needed to revelate.

This old biker haunt may just be the place to do all that and straighten her mind out a little. The owner's wife tried to help with the bag but Dani shot her a look to leave well alone. Settling in to her room she dreamt of what might have been. The times she had spent with Otto working on the motorbikes, learning how to repair the bikes that Morris and her dad had worked on. She wished could have built bikes that had unique customisations on like the sidecar with a car fuel tank in it.

Dani was struggling with her emotions and was starting to feel home sick. She missed Otto. She actually really liked him, he wasn't that much older than her and certainly the age gap was no bigger than the one between Jack and Indy.

The sheets she lay on where crisp and the freshly washed and orchid scents tickled her nostrils. The wife had said the bunk beds are for grubby men you don't want to sleep in those sheets. The thoughts came and went and she drifted off into a world of dreams. Revelating about her life and the desires she has, who she is, who she was and who she will be. A flicker of light and happiness glided into her. This old biker haunt in a sleepy Leicestershire village with the Derbyshire border only a stone throw away, may be the place that changed everything and with that thought she diapered into her dream world.

With only a couple of hours of rest, Dani leapt, startled and shocked, she leapt out of bed, completely naked, her hands up ready to fight, with a cold sweat running down her back. Each breath was loud and her heart beat hard in her chest, slowly she became mentally back in the room. A dream of Tania dragging her by her hair had awoken her, the terror in her mind was all consuming, sickness flowed through her as she regained her senses. A cold feeling crept over her with her hair standing up on her arms, small droplets of sweat clung to them and glistened in the moonlight. The confusion started to disappear as she gathered herself together. The room was dim and the sky was still dark with a nearly full moon hanging in the sky. With only a towel now draped around her she filled the kettle and started making the only thing she felt she needed right now.

The smell of the black coffee, teased her senses, as she turned on the shower. Her playful mind imagined being back in Harz and creating a life, a life far apart from the one she has now, but both incognito from the world.

The towel was old and rough, but the shower was warm and inviting. As the towel fell from her slim waist, her foot slipped into the warm beads of water, the next few moments washed over her, as her skin was warmed by the sprinkling of water bouncing off of her shoulders, the water soaked her hair and ran down her back, over her rounded bottom, down her long slender legs and it now gathered around her feet. As the warmth of the water cleansed her body her mind followed, feeling an escape from the world, secretly disappearing from where she was.

Steam filled the entire room and the mirror misted over, lost in haze of warmth and damp. Edging her way under the shower, the caress of the warm water worked its way across her face and down her breasts. Dani had not felt so relaxed in years. The warm soapy water calmed Dani as she set about her usual routine, first her hair then her arms. She took the shower head from the holder. The warm water ran over her arms and across her stomach. The shower head moved ever closer to her pussy. She parted her legs just enough to allow the water to tease her clit. It felt like the slow caress of a giving lover. The shower head lingered as the water created a feeling that bubbled inside. Her clit swelled as the slow pace awoke, not just her pussy but her entire body. The feeling of needing an orgasm, was now gaining momentum. Dani could now feel her lips becoming wetter. She mused at the wetness that felt wetter than water. Her legs parted further, enough to maintain the pressure of the shower head on her clit. She slipped two fingers just inside her pussy. The yearning intensified immediately. Dani leant back against the cold white tiles to steady herself as the rhythm built. Faster and harder she worked her fingers until a tidal wave of pleasure rushed through her. She moved the shower head away swiftly as her clit had become too sensitive to touch, yet she left two fingers inside. She enjoyed the pulsing feeling as her mind and body become focused again. Back to her senses and completely satisfied. Dani reached for the rough white towel and draped it around herself.

The sun shone sweetly through the window at her, as she sipped on her drink. A post orgasmic coffee, allowed her to be lost from the world completely.

Clarity and focus was now running wild in her mind. Control of her destiny felt like it had arrived. Dani was new. Dani was ready to finish and create all in one.

Down in the bar, she radiated confidence, her tight leather trousers squeaked as she sat down and her effortless beauty needed no make up to enhance it. Her breasts poked through the tight white top she wore with no bra, her nipples drawing their own attention as she ordered her food. Sat astride the bar stool she sipped on another coffee. The owner brought over a plate of scrambled eggs and bacon, with a side of thick toast. Presentation was not the aim. A full plate of good tasting food was actually all this guy was trying to achieve.

Dani was not ladylike in any way when presented with breakfast, especially with the appetite her solo shower had created. With her plate cleared, she noticed bikes parked in the pub, she noticed many quirky little details she had missed before. The owner mumbled the words 'you full love?' his way was so friendly and kind, nothing posh nothing pretensions about him at all.

Dani was still looking at the bikes when he said.

"I like having them there, it feels good to see them while I work or have a brew"

He explained how an old couple had visited once and had been inspired by the bikes in the pub, They had said that when they got home they would make a workshop with 50's café theme, then put his workshop in there too. The owners smile was nostalgic as he talked about getting all kind of folk in here. Until a few words hit Dani very hard.

"I hope the couple did it, they would have needed a large door to get that café racer side car outfit in."

As the owner went on to describe a Manx bike with a red frame and a matching side car, describing the young couple as so in love with a young teenage lad who just wanted to talk about building bikes with his dad.

Dani knew that bike and words failed her…Morris had been here with Dotty and her dad. She wanted to ask so many questions but her words prickled in her throat, as the owner cleared her plate and poured her another black coffee. His departing words floored her.

"That lad used to visit here regular on a big old cruiser when he grew up, always in black, top fella too, he liked to be alone just like you!"

Dani was speechless; The owner was now shuffling around tidying up as Dani sat completely stunned, Her dad had been here, her dad was known here. She knew she would return here. She would definitely visit again. But right now she was motionless, whishing she had met her dad. Ridden her bike alongside him. At least have some memories of him.

With her helmet on no one could see the tears forming in her eyes. She walked out confidently but her heart was screaming in pain, her childhood had been stolen. Tania had taken her mum and dad from her.

"That bitch must die!"

Dani's shadows followed her, she was running but she could not hide from the dark gloom attached to her soul. Her heart was stained by her past. The cloudiness of her life haunted her.

With her phone still connected to her headset and the old 1990s music blaring in her ears, she once again begun the all too familiar run to the sun. The run from her pain. The run from her darkness.

The flamboyant temper she had was boiling inside her. The desire for revenge was back. The desire to kill had returned. Her frantic brain felt insane. Dani had no ability to see that revenge might not rid her of her 'daddy issues' but her need to do this, fed her excitement. In her mind the only thing that would help is to finish the list of her dad's and seal it with the torture of Tania.

As the roads paled into insignificance, the torture of her own mind reigned supreme. Her pain was a stain on her life and her soul was slowly bleeding all over it. She needed to take control of her life. Until she reached her goal everything was spiralling around her. Until she had closure she would continue in this reckless state of self-destruction, much like her father had before he found his sanctuary in the Harz mountains.

CHAPTER 8: HARBINGER OF EVIL

The day had grown old and the memories of a journey were already fading, long days in the saddle were not Dani's favourite. She was more fast blast and stop to enjoy the area.

The mission in her head was clear. She had a person she wanted to talk to and one she wanted to kill. And then she could end this, end it for good. The south of England was not a place she knew well. Dani did not enjoy anywhere she didn't already know. She was just north of Portsmouth as she rolled into another biker haunt, she sought them out as they made her feel safe, she had made contact with the reporter she met when she first landed in England. She needed to know where Tania was, she needed to know where she would end this now.

A rather unassuming building with red curtains at the windows, a couple of bikes had parked next to the big colourful metal signs, burgers and all day breakfasts. This place would do she thought. It had been a long day in the saddle barley stopping long enough to eat anything, her stomach was empty and her soul matched, it was early evening now as she needed food.

The building was dull, basic tables and blue chairs that looked like they belonged in a hospital waiting room, she walked inside and there was the reporter she had arranged to meet. He was sat with his all day breakfast and a cup of dandelion tea. She scowled as if a hot pan had spat fat at her; he was the epitome of what she disliked in a man. She looked him up and down and the pretend tea was not the only thing she disliked. He was sat in a tweed suit amongst some bikers and builders. Her face shouted even though her voice was silent, he could see the disgust in Dani's face as she sat down beside him.

"Where can I find that bitch Tania?"

Her voice was hard, no soft inflections or hints of niceness. The reporter smiled and explained I can tell you but I would rather get a clear picture of who you are. The scowl returned. Indy had always referred to this scowl as 'pan face' after a pan had spat oil from the stove, the harsh natural grimace she gave the pan was a glare as if she would fight the hot pan.

He clicked his fingers at the serving staff and they ignored him, in this place he was transparent, his rudeness would not be tolerated either. The staff had dealt with real bikers, not the tweed reporter types. He huffed and walked over to the till to order an all-day breakfast for Dani. He shouted back asking what drink she would like

"Black coffee, always black coffee"

She glared again at his pathetic excuse for a drink that looked like it could be served to a child. On his return with a rocket fuel double shot drink, he spotted the heeled boots she was wearing, when he asked her about them, her reply was stoic.

"Don't' get excited they are not for you".

He asked her what she could tell him about herself. The silence was long and awkward. The glare she was giving him made him shuffle in his seat and sweat in his tweed suit. She broke the awkwardness with a sharp few words, 'You want to know what makes me tick?'

"People don't have power over us, we give it them, hell is something we carry with us, not somewhere we go. Indy always told me you have to love yourself, glow from the inside. Well Tania darkened my glow, killed my parents. Everything starts with how you feel about yourself. My dad apparently said all you have to do is be dynamic...What would Dan do?...I don't actually know, I don't remember him!"

She hated the meandering apathy of this reporter, the feelings bubbled inside her as she tried to sit calmly and get to the information she needed. There were two people she needed info on and right now this smug tweed suited twat was playing games with her. She had no idea if he would run the story as a positive on her, like he had done for her dad or flip it make her look like the evil one. She knew the media would run it whichever way they were told to by the bosses.

"Look, I have been dealt a really shitty hand and any psychologist would tell you I am doing well to be able to function at all, with what has happened to me in my life, I am a perfect reaction to a fucked up situation. I will give you the bare bones of who I am, but I need those two addresses!"

The reporter pulled out his notepad and wrote everything down she said. She explained the feelings she battled with, the lost sense of hope and the pain she carries from having her parents taken from her. The control she had while explaining her story created an icy feeling around her. As soon as the last words she was prepared to give, trickled off her tongue, she finished with two final words.

"The addresses?!"

She held out her hand and stared long and cold at the still perspiring reporter. He handed her a note and on it was two names and the addresses underneath them. With no thanks or pleasantry, she stood up and nodded, with her lips pursed and her heart crying. But her face still remained stern.

The bubble of noise behind her did not penetrate her mind and she strutted confidently past all the old bikers who looked her up and down, they commented on what they would do for a night with her. None of the lewd comments were heard; she had the 1000 yard stare and in her head a mission. She was two stages away from an apocalyptical escape of biblical scale.

As she mounted her bike and started it up, four old bikers were sat eating cake and drinking tea, they all looked up as she started her bike and immediately started revving it. They laughed and commented.

"She will keep going 'till it drops a valve".

The old bikers all nodded and looked away as she started peacocking outside of the café, wheelie, rolling burnouts, rev bombs and the obligatory Hollywood skid.

The cake munching bikers shook their heads again as she repeated these stunts until the police showed up. The blue lights flashed and reflected in the windows of the biker haunt. She only stopped to wait for the car to pull up behind her; this was the moment she wanted. She was taunting the establishment and Tania. Front brake on tight, suspension compressed with her body weight over the front wheel. Black rubber was stripped from the tyre and thrown over the bonnet of the police car. The deed stuck tiny rubber balls of her disgust to the white and blue paintwork of the police car, the faces of the old bikers now cracked a smile, for the first time in the show.

The windscreen was littered with the smoking hot black mess from her tyre, which angered the police. The driver instinctively pulled the wash/wipe stalk in the car and smeared the mess across the entire windscreen. The delight of this mistake created a raucous laughter from the group stood watching the spectacle. Dani did what Dani did best. Dani created a spectacular display of skill, stupidity and reckless behaviour all in one go. She slowly released the front brake and let the bike roar away, the rear wheel gripped on its overheated tyre and lifted the front wheel high, Dani's expert feathering of the throttle, displayed her misspent childhood.

She exited the car park still on her back wheel and screaming what would Dan do? The crowds behind her cheered, they had no idea of the pain she was exercising and the torment she carried. They just saw a woman who could ride better than any of them. One of them chuckled as the smoke settled and the police slowly drove away with the driver sticking his head out of the side window to see, not able to give chase. One of the old cake munching bikers wiped the crumbs from his long greying beard and said;

"Well I would like to borrow her balls for the day!"

The rear wheel of her bike struggled to keep its grip, Dani was in her kamikaze state of mind and nothing could scare her now. She was alive and if she died she would live again, she had watched too many road warrior style films and her fury would not slow. She was beyond the ragged edge of riding. Every traffic light appeared to be on green, every car gave way and every slip of her tyre appeared controlled. As if her guardian angel was riding pillion with her.

Her ear piece inside the helmet, alerted her she had reached her destination and she grabbed a fist full of brakes causing her bike to skid to a stop. Her breathing was rapid and the sweat was starting to run down her face. The hair on the back of her neck was pricked and the skin electrified. This was the closest to collapse she had ever been. She was in no mood for a long drawn out torture. The first name on the list she did not know, the second was Tania. As she read the first name out loud her anger levels raised.

"Angus MacLeod"

She was plotting the execution of a man she had never met, a man who had done her no wrong, a man who was at the top of the food chain. Her eyes were wide and her breath now frantic. She was clearly out of control even for Dani. Her hands shook and legs felt weak. A Scottish voice bombastically gave orders.

"Get that bike in the garage, how many fucking times do I have to tell ya, don't bring the new stock here!"

Without even looking up she clicked the bike into gear and rode it into the garage. It was a sparse garage with only a multi gym in it and a couple of mirrors on the wall. His aggressive voice matched with who she expected him to be. A thief in the night, a bully who was too afraid to do his own dirty work. This guy was a bike thief, whose team of scooter riders went out to mug people of motorbikes at traffic lights. This man disgusted her more than the last she had dealt with up on the hillside in Derbyshire. She had been working down the list in order of disgust. The more they angered her for what they had done, the closer to the end of the list she had wanted them to be. After this thief, it left her with only her dad's killer to deal with. The stakes had gotten higher and her mental state more fraught. She had not expected to feel so damaged by the atrocity's she was creating. She expected to not be shaken by the severity of the destruction she was causing.

As she lifted off her helmet, her hair fell from it. Her face bright red and anger strewn across it. The feeling inside her was raucous and raw, damaged and broken. Surprise and confusion rippled across his entire demeanour and quickly softened. He questioned what do we have here then? She never moved a single muscle. Her gaze was fixed on him and her head hung low, with her eyes peering from below her brow. She calmly asked.

"*Do you take bikes?*"

Her voice was harsh and her tone short, he smiled and explained that he might be able to help, he offered for her to come inside and freshen up. His voice was so sleazy it made her almost vomit over him. He moved closer to her, his breath was burning across her face with the smell of stale tobacco and beer that taunted her nostrils. Dani leant in and whispered in his ear 'death or cake?' His recoil was slow and his confusion fast. Before Dani could even see his face, she stabbed him in the side of his torso, the blade glanced the lower rib, the knife scored the bone with vibration sent through the wooden handle of her knife handle. As he fell to the ground she stood over him. The blade glinted in the florescent light and red sheen dripped to the floor. He tried to stem his own blood flow. His screams did not touch her, the shrill pained noises were dulled. She was numb. She was already dead. Dani was the harbinger of evil and the maker of destiny.

The harsh look on her face stared down at his weak pathetic bleeding mess, as he lay on the floor his face was tortured, the blood flowed between his fingers, his grey face was becoming sweaty. Dani lifted up her high heeled boot and gently placed in on his forehead, the stiletto edge was sharp, the skin started to tear on his forehead as she forced it harder into his brow. Her stinging words told him how despicable he was. The rant was long as she pressed harder and harder down with her heel. The words trickled along his clammy flesh as he begged for her to stop. Her words smashed into his mind, as she explained she was fighting for the downtrodden, his life beat them down harder, his bike theft business was taking from people who had worked hard to achieve. Not like him lying and cheating his way through life.

The balding fat man cried as she dragged her spiked booted down his chest, ripping his now blood stained tee shirt. He begged for his life once again as she stared down at him. The fierce cold stare showed him that her mind was made up. This is where he would die.

She slowly strutted over to the multi gym, the round weight on the leg curl sat with its 30 KG's at rest. Dani was small but strong. The weight slid off the machine and her small biceps bulged. The weight got heavier in her hands as she held it above him, his tears came and he once again begged for his life. The tears and pathetic empty words angered her more as she let go of the weight and dropped onto his forehead. The skull immediately cracked and his cerebral cortex was wide open, blood splattered against the mirrors on the wall and slowly started to track a red path down them.

The round metal clanged and rolled along the concrete garage floor, eventually hitting the garage wall and taking a chunk out of the brickwork too.

Lay motionless but very much alive making slurred noise and dribbling over himself, she had lobotomised him in the most brutal way, she could hear him trying to speak, he could manage no more that inaudible attempts of words that had no meaning. She looked back at him and shook her head in disgust at him.

"Just call me call me Walter J Freeman, Lobotomies fix everything!"

Dani remembered Indy saying her dad had always told Joanne 'you calm my mania and fuel my fire all in one go, we are a match' Joanne used to say 'You raise my fire and clam my pain we are a match, between heaven and hell', they had tamed each other, they were fiery yet tamed. Beast yet soft. Dani was in her fiery stage and needed a calmness, a taming of her anger and a softness to her pain. Indy had always spoken about how Dan had adored Joanne. Dani was always angered that she had never seen them love each other, never had the pleasure of learning to love by watching the perfect couple. She had never seen the way they had looked at each other, never seen the way her dad would protect her mum from anyone, nor had she seen how her mother was the same as him, loving yet fierce. She could protect her man if she needed to, when he was broken she stepped up, when he was strong she allowed him to be more dominant. They worked like Yin and Yang. Indy never told Dani how much she had loved Dan too, she never mentioned that she wished Dan had loved her like she did him. She suppressed her love and was pained every time she saw Dan look at Joanne in the way she wished he looked at her.

Dani was raging; Dani was struggling to keep her composure. Dani needed something to calm her. What she needed was an explosive orgasm.

With her bike parked at the front of a bar, the darkness started to fall. The lights started to shine through and illuminate the streets. She stood drinking sparkling water, the bubbles tickled her tongue and focused her mind. She stood calm on the outside, manic on the inside. She was trying to control her mania, the swirling mess inside her head carried with it many issues and thoughts.

One of the guys who was loud and obnoxious was flashing his cash around buying everyone drinks was now staring at her, he almost drooled as he looked the leather glad Dani up and down, with her bright deadlocks dominating the view as much as her breasts.

She was mentally still a messed up teenager, who was angry at the world, she didn't give a dam about anyone that she hadn't grown up with. The world was putrid to her. She often felt low and never enjoyed anything that wasn't extreme or that she didn't control. She was a growing dominatrix; she just had no idea how kinky her ways were. She liked being seen, but not known, she had no desire for people to know her name.

The drunken arrogant flash suited reveller now moved towards her, trying to impress her with all his best lines, each time he wafted a tired old chat up line her way, she looked at him, squinted and shook her head. The more she looked uninterested the more he tried to impress her. She knew what she was doing; she knew she was controlling him. She stood up straight, no longer leaning on the bar, looked him square in the eyes and said.

"Look, do you wanna fuck? Or dance around me all night?"

A dopy big grin appeared across his face, highlighting his middle aged lines. He practically skipped as he walked, she marched behind him, he stumbled as he walked into his hotel room, tripping over nothing. Dani pushed him on to the bed yanking his trousers off, this was no romantic love making. Dani practically tour his clothes off, yanking on his cock until it was hard. She pulled down her leather trousers and took his dick inside her. She rocked and bucked dragging her nails down his chest, tearing at his skin, his hands went numb under her knees. Her breasts bounced harder and harder the faster she went, she flung her clothes over the bed without stopping, his eyes were wide as he stared and her perfectly formed tits. Nipples that protruded proud bounced in front of him. She could feel them tingle as she pinched them. The praying mantis tattoo nestled between her boobs and coved her chest above them. Her victim was mesmerised, she knew she was in full control and at any moment she could rip off his head like a Mantis does.

The sex had started to calm her and she was on the verge of an orgasm, she leapt off his throbbing erection, and changed to submissive, she bent over the dressing table in front of the mirror and begged to be fucked hard, the harder he thrust the more she wanted, shouting 'spank me' over and over again. Each red mark left on her buttocks heightened the sensation, he grabbed her hair and pulled it hard enough to bring her head back almost to the point of choking her and she loved it, the feeling of being controlled exploded inside her as she writhed, pulling against the restraint he had on her, his large hands gripped tightly around her hair, that was twisted around his fingers, being submissive again only made it feel more intense. Being able to see herself being fucked in the mirror was the crescendo moment for her. As her waves of pleasure ignited inside her, the end of his cock got even harder and he filled her with the warm feeling of cum.

Dani's skin was so intensely feeling every small movement. She draped herself on the bed with her chest beating hard. It was the first time she had let a man be dominant in the bedroom and she had loved it.

His daft expression was back and he was already asking for her phone number and making a fresh pot of coffee. She shook her head and said no words, Dani had taken what she wanted and in her head she had already left the room. With her finger now pointed at her chest tattoo. A large smile started to creep over her face. The smile had evil in it. The smile had darkness in it. The smile had hidden pain in it.

Her following speech was stern, every word cold and haunting, so much so that his face showed his fear. His semi hard cock was now shrivelled into himself as his terror was in full flight. Dani was clearly a harbinger of evil. Her words cut him down mentally faster than his semi erect cock had retracted.

"Fear me for I am more broken than you can imagine"

She sneered at him as she poured her coffee, the fresh smell of the black nectar floated around the room. Dark roasted notes filled her nostrils with her familiar daily excitement.

"I like black coffee or whiskey nothing in between...its 9 pm do you really want a black coffee? Fuck no. Pass the bottle of bourbon I like my whiskey straight, nothing wrong with that!"

He chucked as he awkwardly shifted from side to side, his shrivelled cock still wet from the encounter. He tried to speak and she shut him done hard. The verbal onslaught of attack echoed though his ears.

"You think you are all that and a bag of chips don't you! You think you are a fukin' big deal well let me tell you. You are fuck all without that money. You're a twat! You should have done good for people with that money, not think you own the world and everyone in it!"

His fear reduced as his bravery increased, her insult had bristled him. The true arrogance came out his face which was contorted by his anger; he leaned forward and raised his hand to slap Dani. With his hand raised above her head she threw her fist into his throat. The wind pipe crumpled under her dainty looking knuckles. The noise he produced was like injured sea lion, grasping for air, he fell to the floor with his hands clasped around his throat.

She was looking at herself in the mirror, knowing no one sees her as she is really, no one's knows her, she is just a dirt bag with pent up anger and more emotions that she can handle. The tattoo of her praying mantis was prominent between her pert breasts. This was her spirit animal. A female who was kick ass and took what she wanted.

A glance over her shoulder allowed her to watch the arrogant wanker trying to stand up with one hand still clutching his throat. His cum was just starting to dribble from her and down her leg, she reached into the pocket of her leather jacket, the black leather contrasted with the white sheets raising a smile on her face. She produced the bowie knife. The air around Dani felt cold. The world disappeared, even the room felt like it had left. The blade pierced his pale flesh, diving through his chest with ease, bouncing off the edge of his shoulder blade the other side. The sharp carbon steel hunting knife ripped through his heart, extinguishing him with ease.

A cold corpse lay on the floor with blood pooling around him. Not even a blink of emotion came from Dani as she grabbed his tee shirt that was lay on the chair and wiped his cum from her leg. She tossed it on to him and sat playing with her clitoris.

Her mind drifted away from the room she was in. Back to the mountains. Back to where she felt like home was. She dreamed of being lay next to the stream. A stream she had spent many days playing in. Learning and exploring. This was the place she first fantasised about kissing a boy. Yet here in this haze there was a man in her dreams not a boy. The man she had rebuffed more times than she could remember. These feelings were different now. She no longer dreamed of rebuffing him, she dreamt of him taking her. A man she knew she could trust with her heart and a man she could give her passion too. Her hands started to wonder as her fantasy took over her body. Wet still from the cum she had just taken, she pushed her fingers firmly inside herself. She wanted to feel the pressure of being stretched open. Dreaming about being by the stream with the man she had overlooked wishing he had been her first encounter and her only encounter. Dani was lost, lost in an erotic moment that had never happened. Her fingers played out what her body wanted. Her thoughts dreamt that they were his hands working her pussy and tweaking her nipples. Her lust grew along with her heartbeat. Waves and waves of pleasure ran through her as she arched her back for the final thrust of her fingers. A shudder of delight resonated from between her legs. Slowly it built its way up into her stomach before releasing a full body intense orgasm, that tingled all over her skin and exploded in her mind, as she panted, every fast breath took her closer to her escape from the atrocity she had just committed. She was always just one orgasm away from feeling good again.

Dani was back, but Dani was still so cold, she had used his credit card to order pizza and as she awaited the pleasure of his last meal he did not get to eat. She swigged from the bottle of whiskey and sucked on her wet fingers, the taste of their sex created one last flurry of orgasmic swirling to please her again before falling asleep full of whisky, pizza and cum.

Awoken by a dawn chorus, cheerful notes fluttered through the open window, singing their way into the room. The poetic rhythm of the birds danced around her head, tickling her ears and waking her mind, a sweet smell of happiness flooded through her thoughts, her soul lifted and the shackles of pain were monetarily gone. The focus of her eyes flickered into reality and a rage of darkness flooded her mind. Stood over the now stiff body of yesterday, her mind was fixed on the job in hand as her cold dead victim lay at her feet. She pulled out the cigarettes and lighter from the jacket of the soon to be cadaver. A long drag on two cigarettes at once, she flicked them on to the cum and blood stained bed then left the room with a march of a sergeant major.

Helmet on and thoughts raging in her mind, her blood ran cold and the thud of her heartbeat pounded in her temples. Words bounced around in her mind, phrases she had said, read and heard from the stories of Dan. Her father was a working class hero, a legend a man who was celebrated by the masses. The returning thought powered its way to the front again. Tania took him away. She killed him. It's her fault!

A screech of rubber and growl of exhaust note, left behind a mini inferno just starting to rage in the window above her, as she left with a mind full of words causing her pain again.

The rage built higher and higher as she raced to the route she had memorised, she had rode this route many times in her head over the last 24 hours. She now knew where Tania lived and this was the day she had fantasised about for years, this time she took the journey for real.

Dani was out to take, take back what she had lost, and take what she had. Everyone had always tried to please Dani. All she wanted was to avenge the death of the father she never knew. It's not easy to live when everyone pampers you, it's not easy to live, let alone breathe. Her mind crashed every night as she drank to numb the pain of her childhood. It should have been easy to live with all the love she was given, but nothing eased her darkness, nothing fitted for her. All she wanted was to end this. She had imagined Tania many times stood in a bar thinking she was all that and a bag of chips. This is what had sparked her death fuck to the man in the bar. Whenever she saw this arrogance, the anger built inside her and the words raged around her mind, screaming why don't you fuck off and die. Now it was up to Dani to instigate this vision for Tania.

Visions that she had created from half stories now kicked her thoughts around, images of her dad bleeding on the street and the onlookers who had tried to protect him. With Tania smiling as she had achieved what she thought was impossible.

The ride along this death march in her mind was missed, no memory of it as she ranted in her helmet. Screaming at Tania and the world for the atrocity served to her. The words reverberated off the inside of her helmet for no one else to hear as she ranted to herself.

"Why should I see you when I hate you? Retribution and reckoning needs to be served, Justice must be given. I don't understand why the fuck you even gave a shit about us! You dragged us down into your hate of yourself. You cut me down before my life got started. I will write your obituary in your blood. Who were you to criticise us? You have your vices and problems too. Fuck you bitch, you wanna antagonise me, well you fukin did bitch. I will fuck you up! I am going to fuck your skinny little ass right up! This is my anarchy this in my avengement. This is my moment to shine and be the star in my own life. Step the fuck up bitch, step the fuck up!"

The resentment in her soul led her on. The knowledge that Tania had not been brought to justice over her dad's murder, caused her to see nothing but Tania's pain, Tania's suffering and Tania's death.

The burn of pain surrounded Dani, It stabbed at her heart and ripped through her soul. It had torn her life in two. Pain had been a friend to her, all of her life. Pain had sat with her daily for so long she had realised her pain's name was grief. Misery had encompassed her very being. Now it was time to exorcise her pain, her grief and her misery.

Dani stood outside of an overly neat house, with simple fittings and nothing soft about it. The most functional beige house she had ever seen. No flowers, no vibrant colour and certainly nothing but beige curtains hanging at the sides of the windows.

The neat gravel path crunched with every step, sickness filled her throat, cold sweat ran down her back and adrenaline engulfed her body, causing a tremble to run though her hands. The short path she was stood on had brought her to a plain door, with a camera style door bell. She had no intention of alerting Tania to her presence, she had waited for this moment her whole life. She had wanted to stand here longer than she had been able to ride a motorbike. This moment was her crescendo. Every step of her journey the last few weeks had been building to this. Today was the day of reckoning. Today was her redemption. Today was her moment of glory.

The temperature was cold to her, even though the sun shone bright in the sky. The people passing by wore tee shirts and no coats, yet she stood in front of her salvation ice cold. The adrenaline fuelled tremor in her hand silenced. Slowly Dani opened the door, her helmet still on and her senses on full alert. This was a moment to savour, a moment to absorb every detail and this was defiantly not a moment to rush.

As Dani stepped into the house she could hear loud classical music blasting out, every step she took, felt like a huge step, until she saw Tania stood with her back towards her. Tania was exposed with a vulnerable stance, as she carefully changed the vinyl record that had been playing, the room had become silent. Dani silently standing subdued. The moment had come, the moment was here, the moment was nigh. A stern and angry voice said.

"Hello Tania, remember me?"

The slightly muffled by the helmet voice attacked Tania ears, causing a violent spin to be face to face with two bikers dressed in black and stood side by side, one larger, with heavily worn leathers and a black helmet, the other hourglass figure, with tight fitting leathers and a white helmet. Dani launched forward and head butted Tania, splitting her nose across her face and knocking her out cold. Dani spun round to catch a glimpse of what she thought was a person stood next to her. As she lifted her visor, there was no one else in the room. Dani was convinced someone had been stood there, a flash of a person disappeared as she turned to look.

Slowly she removed her helmet, her red hair, gently cascaded from the white lid and echoed the blood that was now pouring from the unconscious face of Tania. Dani was becoming what she had imagined, she was avenging her dad, she was avenging the infamous Revelator. Dani sat patiently on the sofa opposite Tania, looking at her work and revelling in the bloody mess she had started. Tania lay with blood congealing on her abused face. Dani had restrained her hands and ankles with duct tape and was now sat drinking a very strong black coffee, contemplating her avengement.

Nearly an hour had passed and the blood on her white helmet was now dried on equally as much as the disfigured face which was covered in equally dry crimson pain. A gentle moan started to work its way across the room. Tania still not fully conscious had started to wriggle, unknowing bound with silver 'gaffer tape' Dani smiled, sipping at her now cooling brew.

This was it, this was her time, this was the moment she could right the wrongs given to her.

A huge gasp of breath with eyes wide open, Tania was now once again face to face with Dani. Fear and shock rocked the ice maiden as she tried to wriggle free of her binding's. For the first time Tania no longer had control, no longer had the upper hand nor the ability to protect herself.

Dani did not speak, she did not even look Tania in the eye. She slowly enjoyed her decadent artisan black nectar. Tania demanded to be set free, but Dani still did not communicate. Dani refused to her look up at her, this was the moment, the true power shift was felt by the crooked cop.

With an empty cup Dani stood up, placing her used mug on the gloss black table next to the coaster, she had allowed the drink to dribble down the side leaving a ring on the gloss black glass table. Tania was immediately triggered and started to rant at Dani about her mess and disregard of rules. No rush was returned, no fluster and no panic. A small gun was however returned and gently placed in-between the teeth of her nemesis.

"Shut the fuck up bitch, it's my turn!"

The voice was cold and hard like the gun she held. She explained to Tania.

"My father's life and my mother's was taken by you, in that moment you started a ripple effect bigger than you can imagine, ruining my life before I could even sit up on my own, or remember my parents smiles. Now I will avenge them, I will take you away from your loved ones just as you did to me!"

Tania was silenced by the onslaught of Dani, the words were sharp and angry, more angry than Tania had heard before in her career. Dani was different she was carrying evil. The old Tania was still there as she started her attack.

"Take me away from my loved ones! I have no loved ones. Lone bitch that's who I am. So fuck you and your dad's faded reputation. A has been who never was!"

Dani's rage hit the proverbial red line, the gun was dragged from Tania's yellow coffee stained teeth chipping one of the front teeth as it dragged it way out of a clenched jaw. Dani lifted up her foot and smashed it into Tania's face. The already split nose crumbled under her boot, the remains of the bone, shattered, leaving a flat drooping sack of skin and more blood pouring from her already bruised face. Dani stood panting, rage circling around her and sweat running down her back. The anger levels were off the scale and she could not decide what to do. Kill her now or torture her? The two thoughts raced around filling her with a raged confusion. The melee of thoughts caused a dizzy sensation to attack her. A staggered moment and a lack of clarity showed her struggle as she rocked from foot to foot with Tania slumped on the floor held by her bindings. Tania could see the weakness and the lack of strength she had.

"Your nothing like your dad, he was the strongest man I had ever met. Yet he still fell before me! He was crazy, a danger and he needed to be stopped."

Tania chuckled her words with the pain of her broken face still contorting her expression. Through the pain she attacked Dani with words designed to destroy her mentally, rip her mind in two and collapse her wellbeing. Tania had taken down many a stronger person this way.

Dani's life had been spent every day not wanting to wake up and her life had been fucked before she started it. She never wanted people around her, often wanting to rip the head off of anyone who tried to be in her personal space. Her mind was full of bullshit stories that did not replace her parents. Her rage was back, her dizziness gone and her steely gaze returned. She spoke clear and precise.

"Take that back bitch. You don't know my dad, you don't know me!"

A bloody, pained and contorted smile rippled across Tania's face, showing her chipped blood covered teeth. She shook her head and laughed at the words Dani had said so sternly said to her. Tania returned her monosyllabic strong response *'No'*.

Dani lifted her chin and sneered at her pain, her problems and the reason she had started her tour of avengement lay beneath her. Dani felt suffocated and didn't care of the damage she was causing to herself, she was in self-destruct mode. She had lost sight of her life. No hope and her sanity was broken. Cold to the world and no longer focused on anything but this moment, her mind was fed on the chaotic life she had tried to make sense of. Nothing had ever been fine. Nothing had ever settled. Nothing had ever made sense. Her mind had cried its entire life. This was her life laid bare. Her only mission now lay on the floor bleeding in front of her.

The steel of the gun was heavy in her hand and her thoughts clearer than they had ever been. A moment of euphoria started to swim within her. She felt the destiny rise before her, nothing else mattered just the vengeance her dad needed to gain.

A cheeky voice rippled its way through the house, as the door at the rear of the building clicked shut.

"Hi hunni...where are you? You were right, we should try again."

Tania's ex walked in to the room almost skipping with happiness to see Tania again. A smile of delight rippled across the face of the Avenging Revelator.

"So you must be Liam."

Horror and fear struck Liam, to the point of a childhood fear of the dark. He was a weak man that had always been controlled by Tania. He was bullied and downtrodden, always returning to her, she never loved him, she just loved to control him. He was the closest thing to love she had ever managed. Tania was a woman who walked alone and had a deep buried fear of someone always watching her, a dread that someone was always there, breathing down her neck and the closest thing to comfort was her punch bag Liam.

Tania's only comfort, the closest thing to experiencing feelings was now creating a pool by his foot as the child like fear ran down his leg creating a dark stain in his blue jeans.

The thud bounced into Tania's ears before the sound of the gun. The vision of her failed attempt of trying to love, fell into his own wet pool of fear. Along with it any hope of love developing in her heart of stone. The single shot fired had struck him in the side of the head and left the bullet lodged in the rear of his brain. For the first time ever Tania cried, Tania had a feeling of pain and terror now. Her anguish laid bare in front of Dani. She revelled in seeing Tania's pain on her blood stained face and the first tears she had let go since preschool trickled along the damaged face of Tania.

"That's the vengeance for my mum, my dad's will return for you."

Strong thumbing boots stomped out of the house leaving a wake of new pain running down the disfigured face of the ice maiden. Dani did not want to kill Tania in this moment; she had avenged her mums death. Killing her now would not avenge her father too. Leaving Tania to suffer and fear her would build the climax she wanted to create.

CHAPTER 9: MORALS

Red and orange hues shimmered through the trees as the sun dropped once again, another 24 hours of her life started to draw to a close. Each day that ticked by was another day lost forever. Dani's mind swirled with questions. Questions that challenged her very existence and the every decision she had made.

She toyed with the thoughts, was she doing right? Was she just as bad as Tania? Was she making her dad proud or not?

Her questions were shattered as a loud exhaust note fired, shaking the ground and causing her flesh to prickle. Anger and confusion rattled around inside her. There he was, the biker she kept seeing, dressed in black, with a black visor and black helmet. He threw a leg over a black naked bike and screamed away with his front wheel off the ground and his rear light now glaring back her. The confusion and anger dissipated fast and was replaced by the need to know who kept appearing and watching her? Who was keeping an eye on her? Who was trailing her every movement?

The thoughts slowed as she chased the rear light along the road. But before she could get into to 3rd gear the red light had disappeared into the distance. She was alone on the road and now aimlessly chasing nothing in the darkness. At first she thought it could be Jack, but this guy was bigger, broader across the shoulder and no beer belly.

As she slowed to a more sedate speed her feeling of alienation matched her estranged life. She was alone in life as much as she was alone on a dark road right now. She had left her sanctuary, never feeling settled anywhere, she was destined to roam.

Her only escape was once again her only direction in life, roaming on is all she knew at this point. The paradise of life was being illuminated by her headlight into a sea of black, she found it hypnotic to ride her bike in the dark, the dangers, the success, the escape into the beauty from the zombie wasteland of society. She looked for a place to sleep, eying every discreet looking area. She was used to sleeping in the woods, growing up in Northern Germany. She had often tried to escape her pain with motorbike trips out into the forests. Completely self-sufficient and solo.

With her roll mat laid out behind a dry stone wall, she pondered another cold night, wild from the world. Her friends appeared in the form of a flask off coffee and a hip flask of whiskey. She drank nothing in between these two drinks. Only the time of the day dictating which she drank. Life was simply coffee to wake and whiskey to sleep. Revelations flowed in to the evening, her tiny bit of paradise away from the apocalyptic world she despised, just like her father had done before her. A tarp was pulled tight above her and the warmth of her drink was her tiny bit of safety, like the paternal hand she never had, rested on her shoulder as she drifted off to sleep.

Her slumber had crept in as she sipped from her flask, whishing she knew the feeling of a proud parent.

No matter who had tried. Nothing would ever come close to the parental pride she desperately wanted to experience.

Once again the cycle restarted, her bleary eyes peeked through the whiskey haze she was all too often in. A misty morning starting to brighten her world as she looked along the dew drop grass. The coffee in her other flask was now cold and made her grimace as she tried to swig at it. The bleary thoughts led her emotions to be at the forefront of her clunky feelings. She pulled out the lists she had in her inside jacket pocket, the lists from Dan, of who he wanted to avenge and who deserved what. The more she read the scribbles on the back. The more she saw a man suffering with his own mind. Struggling to keep his mind in check and battling with his desires.

Her mind was awash with the need to hug her father, cuddle in to the bosom of her mother and feel protected like a child should.

A thought still blurred by the drinks of last night tortured her into wanting food and a black coffee to hide the pain she was always aware of. The ride into the town had felt sketchy and the sensation of her safe haven was not as strong as normal.

Sat in a small café a young man brought over a plate of scrambled eggs and large mug of coffee. The sensational smell invigorated her and the next 10 minutes where a blind assault on the food and drink she had in front of her. Nothing else in the café had been seen. Nothing had been heard and nothing had been witnessed. Sitting back in her chair revelling in the feeling she had. Delighted by the warmth of feeling full and content once again. She noticed the barista. His face was still but his expression was shouting at her.

He tried to stutter some words out but to no avail. He tried to alert her to something but no words came, he just pointed an index finger to the floor next to her. She looked disgusted at him and despised weak men. Just as she turned to look at the floor where he pointed his words came.

"The old biker...but there was two...not seen him in years...only comes when people sit here in times of despair"

Lay on the floor was a leather bound old book, with loose papers wedged between the pages. The barista went on to tell her how; the old biker was a legend here. Last time he had seen him, it was to visit a young hippy woman who sat exactly where you are now. Only this time there was two of them.

Dani's stern expression overpowered her emotional look, her red bulging teary eyes still gave her pain away as she asked what the bikers looked like.

"Both in black leather, one old and clean shaven the other younger taller and broader with an unkempt greying beard, I had heard that a duo of bikers had been appearing recently rather than one around here"

Shock struck Dani…could this have been Morris and her dad, she grabbed the book and locked the front door of the cafe. She demanded a large coffee and said you need to tell me everything you know about the two old bikers. The barista smiled and said I think I actually recognised the bigger one, now I think about it. He once saved my life when I was being attacked in this very shop.

Sitting beside Dani, The young man took a deep breath. A smell of coffee and cinnamon raced around his nostrils. Dani had no such experience, no fragrances danced merrily around her nose. Hyper focussed yet confused, her franticness exploded as she pawed through the pages.

The barista spoke of a time that the larger biker had burst into the shop while he was being savaged by a gang of thugs, they had abducted a woman, beautiful hippy type on a custom Harley he exclaimed. Dani was frowning she knew this story, as the helpful coffee maker continued it was obvious this was Indy he was speaking of, the story went on to explain how this biker burst in, attacked the man who had been torturing him and killed him.

"Saved my life I am sure of it"

A lump balled in her throat, this had to be a story of her dad. The thought wreaked havoc in her mind. The thoughts bounced around her skull, kicking around the dark abyss of Dani's mind.

'My dad fought for the righteous and the good, extinguishing the evil of society. Now it's my turn to avenge them.'

The man of coffee sat back and said how he never got to say thank you, know his name or tell him his name. The badge on his apron said Tom. Dani took a moment to digest his name, remember him and consider the respect Tom had for Dan.

Tom sat forward in his chair and leant in far closer than Dani would have liked, only the fact that her dad had saved his life, stopped her from launching a scathing attack on him for being so close. Tom's voice lowered, far lower than she expected. His more gravel noted voice scratched across the table towards her. The words slowly marched into her ears as the story was told.

Each word of the story brought with it a revelation and an emotional hit of pain. The words weaved around as Tom explained the legend of the old biker who always turned up when someone was down on their luck. Many a troubled person have walked through them doors, more often than not looking for a coffee and biscuits holding a single bank note. One person in particular told me how they had been contemplating suicide down at the dock, ready to take a last drink of vodka before they jumped. An old man pulled up on his old motorbike and side car, offering him a lift. He talked to him for hours, stopped him from doing the unthinkable by the side of the water, before dropping him off here. After giving him some money he sent him in this shop and told him to say, Morris brought me here and said you would look after me. At this point when the troubled man said this, the shop was full of people, the room had gone silent as everyone in the cafe knew old Morris, knew his story and that of his son. Dani's eyes bulged with pained red sorrow, the story was of the two men she never knew but had wanted to know so much. The barista continued his story. Just as I poured him a cup of hot coffee there was nothing but red tail lights illuminating the window as the side car outfit roared passed. I explained why everyone was staring and who Morris was, how he had killed himself on that dock to save his son. The troubled man sat and cried and everyone took it in turns to offer support. They all had a story to tell of Morris. My manger gave him a job after Morris dropped him here and now he is assistant manager. Good ol' Morris at it as ever. Tom stood up and laid a hand on her shoulder and left her with the words.

"If he left that book and he brought the other guy, you are clearly very special in this world. I have never seen them together before, nor leave anything behind"

Dani's furrowed brow ached as she fought back the tears. Taking her time to close the book and carefully re open it at the start. The opening page was neatly written with the words 'Find a place to live by a moral code, the code of Valhalla' written in the top corner was the words 'Dani means god is my judge (Dottie's mantra)'

Her mind was struggling to comprehend this was her dads hand written notes, a mantra of life, a paradigm to live by. As she slowly turned the pages there were moralistic rules of life on each page and hand written notes, some showing inventions, some were rants about society and others love letters to Joanne.

As Dani worked her way through the book making her own notes, she felt closer to her dad than ever before, the Norse style life messages invigorating her and exciting her soul. This was the book of Dan.

The world around her had slipped away, she no longer smelt the coffee, she no longer heard the barista cleaning and she no longer saw the sunlight shining outside. The words merrily bounced around her soul as she learned of the rules of life according to her dad.

One sentence in particular stood out to her;

Honour these lifestyle revelations daily. As she read on the words embraced her like a hug from a father.

1. *Be a person of worldly intelligence, limited scope or narrow experiences will taper your success.*
2. *Travel often, make no judgement, only revelate on what you see. Learning from other cultures is key.*
3. *Fear never leads to glory, only purpose and strength leads your desire, you make the difference, no one else.*
4. *Goals are achieved by rising early, not sleeping like a sloth.*
5. *Speak usefully or be silent. A fool speaking learns nothing.*

6. Age comes to us all, don't wait for it before you start to live.
7. Never trust a friend who is only ever pleasant. A friend will tell you the ugly truth and let you grow together.
8. What will you leave behind, how did you make this world better?
9. Boastfulness attracts misfortune, live humble. Quiet and confident.
10. Moderate yourself ruthlessly, greed will only cause you pain and sorrow.
11. Do not be fooled by wealth, it's an unreliable friend.
12. Your best friend is common sense, a companion many do not have.

The ideology of her dads morals, sat her up straight with tears in her eyes, the glassy look of her pupils illuminated by the deep red setting sun, which now poured through the window, she had been here the entire day and the sign on the door had remained in the closed position. The last few hand written words had hit her hard, a sucker punch to her heart.

My best friend is Joanne, the love of my life...the girl I always should have been with. The girl I shall marry...

Location for proposal: Bodiam Castle

Ring: Ruby solitaire diamonds on the band

Ring bough: Hidden in tool box

Date to propose: 29th July

Plan wedding: TBC

Married: TBC

Live as one in the Harz mountains: TBC

Explore the world together: TBC

A single tear rolled its way down her cheek and the pang of pain smashed into her again, her dad had started writing the list and had written completed next to the ones he had achieved, another tear followed as the realization marched through her mind, nothing was wrote next to the actual proposal. They died before he could actually ask her mum to marry him, he even had the ring and a location set to propose.

Soft words floated passed her neck, awarmth hugged her from behind.

"Morris and Dotty always said only god can judge you and none of us are God"

Her recoil was fast and it shocked the barista as he saw the long bearded biker stood behind Dani and Morris stood in the doorway. The larger biker was crouched over whispering in to the ear of Dani. She sat motionless, unable to move as more words tickled along her neck.

"Dani I am already proud of you. You make me privileged to be your dad with everything you do. I have been by your side every day trying to guide you"

Full blown tears erupted from her tired eyes, as she spun around knocking over her chair, all that she saw was two grubby white feathers falling to the ground, a hint of oil and petrol wafted across her senses in the air. That was the first time she had heard her dad's voice other than being a baby. She had now heard a voice she could remember. The tears came thick and fast as she slumped onto the floor and wailed her emotions into the lonely café.

Tom picked up his phone and text Joe 'Dan's daughter is here, come now'

CHAPTER 10: REVELATING THE PAST

The silent assassin rolled up outside the café, a mocked bike that served its purpose well, a bike that was almost silent parked in the darkness. Joe sat on his bike looking at the young woman crying on the floor. Joe switched off his silent machine and not one person had heard him arrive. His boots made more noise on the pavement than his bike had. Invisible to the world just as he liked. A ghost of society, that no one could find, no matter how hard they tried.

The door creaked as it opened and Dani stood up and was ready to fight. A chuckle came from the stranger before he told of a man he once knew.

"I once knew a man who had that look when startled, I served in Iraq with him, a man who was always ready to protect. His name was Dan!"

Dani's eyes widened and her mouth opened, no noise came from her, the blotchy puffy red face shouted her pain at him. He spoke fondly of Dan and how Dan looked after him when he joined the Military. He taught me so much and saved my life more times than I can remember. Dani was in awe of Joe who clearly knew her father well and had served with him for over a decade.

Joe continued well into the night telling nostalgic stories of her Dad. He had a huge smile as he spoke of his military days with Dan, especially how when Dani was born. Joe was delivering parts to his old mate Greaser and he saw Dan disappear into a bunker with a little baby in his arms. Dani choked and her eyes burned with pain trying to hold back her emotion.

"Dani, Jack has us all looking for you, to protect you and get you out the country…but from what he says you have a list to complete."

She nodded and he passed her the keys of his silent electric bike. He explained this will allow you to get close to anyone you choose without alerting them with a loud exhaust. Dani was sceptical of an electric bike, knowing her dad would disprove of it.

The stories came thick and fast, telling of how your dad would do whatever it takes to achieve his goal, even if he did not like the way he was doing it. Joe's eyes were alight with every word he spoke of Dan. He often welled up telling the stories. With his voice now much more sombre and precise.

"I have a book here that Dan had hand written, he was so well read it was incredible, have a look. I didn't understand half of it really. Dan was always searching

for something. I am not sure even he knew what he was looking for."

Dani's eyes were wide, her hands trembled as her entire body felt ice like to her, she was softened by anyone who had been close to her dad. Her usual aggressive style waned and she waited patiently for the book to be passed to her.

The book was old worn black leather with a pen attached…a pen her dad had used. The edges of the pages were gold coated and the corners of the cover were heavily worn.

As the book touched her hands, a wave of happiness shot through her. A wave of delight and a melancholy feeling engulfed her.

Joe gestured to the barista to leave and he placed a bottle of whisky with two glasses on the table as he went. Dani didn't even register. The smell of the old pages wafted up her nose and exacerbated her feelings. This was her dad's view of the world. The opening quote was immediately setting the scene for the book.

'In this zombie mass media led apocalypse waste land, it's time to rise up scathed and battered, this barren world of selfish pretend love needs me to knock it sideways'.

The first few pages all went on a similar vein, before explaining the terror her father had as a child, being visited by spirits and even ending up wrestling with one that tried to put a pillow over his face. Some of the stories written on the pages brought a cold shudder to her as she had also experienced many visitations from what she thought may be dreams. The faces trying to talk to her on a nightly basis were identical to her dad's stories. One quote stood out, *'Don't trust the sprits who appear to know you, they can just be masquerading to cause harm.'*

Dani had gone pale and her hands were shaking when Joe sat back and lit a large cigar, as he smoked it he ran his figures through his long grey beard and then poured her a glass of single malt.

"This was your dad's favourite, port wood finish this one"

She lifted up her head, with visons of her father she felt closer to her dad than ever. The glass of port wood finish single malt was in a heavy, crystal cut glass, a sharp intake of breath followed as a warm hug wrapped it's way around her. The next few hours became more blurred as she read about her dad's thoughts on the world. The words made sense of who he was and who she was, the parts she was struggling with seemed to make more sense, as her eyes became heavy, she struggled to stay awake and the last few words of the book hit her hard:

Life is just a thin veil over the reality of the darkness in the universe. Humans are the evil and the good (finding the good and eradicating the bad from your day to day is the trick to happiness) However our pain cannot be escaped as its within us, we are the creators of our own pain.

We need to learn how to repair ourselves, meandering apathy is the cancer of understanding. Good virtue breeds this, vices are easy but don't make us happy long term, they actually make the problems worse (think the effect poor food and sugar has upon on us, let alone drugs and alcohol, everything in moderation)

Revenge brings a swift happiness but it is soon replaced by guilt and pain, this needs to be reserved for those that have done inconceivable atrocities to us, not the tiny insignificant wrongs, they must be ignored. Bad decisions cause our own problems. Vices are the lust that make us desire to chase the next goal rather than be happy with what we have.

Chasing false idols is like being hungry and the food being placed slightly further away each day, so you are forever chasing and never being happy, desire is a tortured hell. We need to do right and make good decisions to create our own paradise. If it will help you, do it. If it won't then don't.' The fear is not knowing what will help long term and what wont. Listen hard enough and you will hear the answer. Be distracted and you can't hear.

I have only pain and demons behind me, Lucifer himself stands behind me. I need to shed this past.

The morning light shuffled its way across the floor of the café, the warmth of the rays started to caress Dani's face. Stirring momentarily she was imaging being back in the Harz mountains hoping to see Indy and Otto. A warm green fleece blanket lay across her shoulders as she slowly shuffled to an upright position. Joe was making fresh coffee and opening the shop.

"Sorry Dani, I need to open up ready for the customers, My two guys are not on shift until later"

A story from last night tiptoed through her mind, Joe is the owner and he was the one who gave the troubled guy Morris sent here a job. The pieces of the puzzle in her mind forever mixed up yet making more sense. Joe placed a plate of pastries and a black coffee on Dani's table before sitting next to her. He laid the keys for his silent bike next to the food. The rich cinnamon scent which floated around her made her smile sweeter than she had for years.

"Dani who is it you need, to give you peace? Is it that bitch Tania?"

With a mouthful of pastry she nodded and stared deep into his eyes, the cold ice of her hate spiked and sent a chill right through Joe.

Joe suggested she borrowed his electric bike to surprise Tania. Dani was unsure about the new electric bike.

"Dani what would Dan do?...What would your Dad do?"

Heat rose through her spine, with her mouth still full of breakfast she grabbed her mug and took a huge gulp of black nectar. She slammed the cup on the table wiped her mouth with the back of her hand.

"Thank you Joe I owe you."

With that she marched out munching more food before starting the soundless bike. The lack of vibration and noise was eerie. She pictured arriving with no pomp or circumstance to avenge her father for good. This was her swan song, this was her blaze of glory, this was the crescendo she had been waiting for.

As she rode away with nothing but a slight hum from the motor and a ripple from the tyres on the tarmac. Dani's mind went into a fast cycle, viewing memories from her child hood, dreams she wished were real and the wounds that would not heal bled all over her. The broken mind of an orphan who had her parents removed from her was akin to war time death.

The pain raged inside her, consuming her and pulling her deep in the depth of her dark soul. Searching for her beginning she was struggling to make sense of her world. A feeling she had felt many times before, feeling insecure about herself and her life. Making no progress on her life at all. The pain was a distraction and a reaction to her life. She was haunted by ghosts of what might have been and now she stands alone once again.

Trees, walls and roads had all settled behind her and none of them seen at all. Dani's focus was not right. She knew she needed a place to revelate, to gain her direction and calm her mania.

Silently she rode between two large black ornate wrought iron gates. Leaves kicked up by her tyres with no one hearing her. She parked next to a secluded gravestone with the words covered in aged moss. They read: Here lies the body of Morris. May you dance with Dotty across time for ever.

Dani laid her gloves on the old stone just above the words. The sharp intake of breath felt like fire and her face was stern. The wind blew the leaves around her feet. The trees around groaned and the moment felt solitary.

"Morris, what would dad do?"

Fear had sunk into her, fear of not pleasing her father or finishing his work, the breeze blew straight through her and chilled her to the bone.

"I feel alone. I don't know what to do. What would Dan do? I never knew either of you. All I do is hide from the hell I have"

Time stood still and the trees danced around her, a swirl of emotion flooded her thoughts. Dani turned away from the gravestone and sat on the damp floor, with her head hanging down. The shadow of her life shrouded her in darkness. She had never had cards or flowers from her parents. Never felt the embrace of a parent. The shadow of this fact left a stain in her life. One that could not be washed away.

The blackness paraded over her and she felt every stain of her life. Every time she slowed or relaxed the pressure of her own mind became unbearable. The tears came thick and a small whimper echoed across the empty cold air. Her memories had consumed her and she picked her tormented soul apart. She had never been safe from her own wounded existence. Dani raised her head to see a large woman stood close staring at her. The woman was completely motionless and clearly carried her pain with her too. Her voice was sombre and croaked as she stifled her tears.

"No one notices when a star goes out, billions of others carry on to illuminate the sky. If your star is missing you know, even if the rest do not."

Dani returned no words, a pensive look made her look hard and callous. Dani wasn't looking for person to console her, show her love or affection. The woman turned and walked away muttering to herself as the words whistled over her shoulder.

"Dan would fix it. That's what your dad would do"

Voices came from all around her.

"Make yourself proud and you will make me proud"

Stood tall looking wildly around her into a silent grave yard, there was no body to be seen, not a single person, her hair flicked from side to side as she spun around trying to find whose voice it was, until two grubby white feathers fell in front of her with a smell of petrol and oil intoxicating her once more. Creating a smile. A knowing. A direction. This was it.

She had come so far she could not change direction, she had to finish what she had started and all the pieces were lined up. She hadn't cared how this would end for her. But like most people, she wanted to make her dad proud. She had to finish his work and return to the Harz mountains and live out her parents dreams for them. She missed the life she had there and hadn't realised how much love she had left behind. She was blinded by her pain. The last few days of revelations, had made her feel closer to her dad's memory than ever. She wanted her old life back, but a better version of it. Her new life had to be in the knowledge that she had avenged her revelations.

Subdued, silent and stoic. The silent assassin of a bike gently passed through the old black gates, back onto the road. At the entrance her end had begun.

CHAPTER 11: AVENGE THE PAIN

A feeling of sadness had plagued Dani since the graveyard, a washed out emptiness surrounded her. Nothing pleased her and nothing excited her. Stood in a supermarket with the business of life running around her. People rushed and people ran around doing the daily eat sleep repeat routine. Dani needed something to lift her up and raise her emotional state back to a stronger place. Each day she had been away from Harz had caused her to feel weaker and weaker.

Dani stood with her food and her 'pick me up', dressed in her black leather gear and her neck gaiter still pulled up over her nose. Incognito was her favoured look, hiding from the masses, getting ready to lift her mood. Changing hair styles or colour always made her feel better. A box of red hair dye was just what she needed before she went for the final flight, nothing boosted her mood like her hair looking tidy, her red had started to show routes and she needed to feel perfect for what she was about to do. The mission to end all missions. Her swan song.

The person in front of her was laying items on the conveyer a belt, nothing of any excitement and clearly a family shop. The woman behind started to tell Dani off, started to order her to put her items on the conveyer belt, even though the person in front was still laying items out.

"Come on put your stuff on the belt, I want to get mine on!"

Dani was enraged to be rushed when it would not speed the process up at all. Slowly she turned to face the large woman, a scruffy woman in a baggy kitted red cardigan. Stood facing the rude woman, she glared. Grotesquely she gestured once again for Dani to hurry up, the person in front was still laying out her weekly shop and Dani was in no rush to crowd the person in front of her, no amount of impoliteness here would speed up this process. As hard faced and as angry as Dani was, the person in front had done no wrong, this ugly soul behind her was causing a problem for no reason.

Dani looked the obnoxious woman behind her up and down, before turning away to wait, she had no need to rush and nor has she any right to rush the person in front of her.

From the side of view, Dani saw the shopping separator being tossed passed her and blocking the persons things from being put out including Dani's few items. The woman behind was actually just throwing her things onto the conveyor belt now. The person in front was so overly polite and just asked them to move their things back, so he could finish unloading his items, the polite man was dressed in very dull clothes with his hair cropped neat and a short his face framed by stubble beard. The items were begrudgingly moved slightly backwards from behind, with lots of huffing and puffing and with hardly any extra room made, clearly not enough for all the shopping to be laid out.

Dani's three figures were raised, her heart was now racing as fast as she liked to ride. Her chest felt like it would explode.

"You rude fuckin' bitch, this guy is just trying to unload his family shopping!"

A face of disgust came from behind her and a torrent of abuse followed. Dani stood still, no movement, no more words, nothing but her heavily beating chest to give her anger away. Dani lifted up her heavy black boot and kicked backwards connecting with the woman's knee. A scream of pain echoed around the shop, as the woman fell to the floor. Dani spun around stood once again motionless looking at the pained hideous creature below her. Her large breasts now heaving in a tight white top in her half unzipped jacket as her heart raced with adrenaline and anger fuelling her.

Dani was still holding in her arms the things she intended to buy, she lifted her boot up again, the weathered old leather in need of a polish added to the grungy look she had. The boot came crashing down on the woman's knee once again, sending her pain off the scale as she passed out. With no words, Dani threw her items at the now unconscious rude woman and left with just one item in her hand. Tossing a single note on to the conveyer belt to pay for her one item. A confident strut showed her no fucks attitude. A stomp of a walk as she passed the staff. No one dared challenge her. She had what she needed. The red hair dye for her final blood bath day of reckoning. The end was nigh.

A fresh morning held a mist in the air, a slight fog and dampness floated around Dani's fresh hair. It was pillar box red, her hair always helped her mind set. Today was a cold day, not just in the air but in her heart, her mind and her soul iced her to the core. This was a day of reckoning, a day of retribution and a day of avengement. The payback for her dad. She had already started with the avengement of her mum. Today was personal. Toady was the day of revelations. Today was the end she had planned.

The bike was silent. The electrical bike was not her first choice of excitement, it was quick and she loved that, but she liked the old school ways of internal combustion. It was what her father would have wanted and that thought was always strong in her mind.

A small wine from the motor, a rear tyre struggling for grip on the cold tarmac and Dani was gone, whistling though the roads with the motor wound up hard. Dani was focused, but an odd feeling of being lost was trailing her. She didn't feel lost, she felt as if she knew exactly what she was doing, as usual her mixed up emotional state taunted her.

A wide open road and route she had travelled before, all rolled by in a bright flash as the mist lifted and made way to a bright sunshine which illuminated her way.

The almost silent bike rolled along a small dirt path, lots of loose gravel and dust flicked up hitting the bottom of her bike, until she came to a very slow, subdued and subtle stop. The bike was waiting active and silent, the perfect escape from her mission.

A small slabbed area with very neat edging and no flora to be seen. Simple and precise with nothing fluffy. As Dani tried the door it was predictably locked. Dani had as ever a solution for every problem, on her last visit she had taken the key from Liam's pocket. The key turned smoothly and the door silently opened. She stepped inside to see a TV playing and Tania's feet in view through the kitchen doorway.

Dani took a moment to savour her feeling and a large feeling of pride swept through her, today would be a good day, the first day of the rest of her life.

The air smelt of bleach and the house was impeccably tidy, with slate coasters neatly pilled on the side in a small wooden sleeve. Dani took two slate coasters very quietly from the holder and clenched her jaw as she prepared herself, this was all out war. Tania's face was horror-stricken, still with bandages on her damaged features. Dani launched into the room. She threw one of the slate coasters at Tania, which caught her in the cheek tearing open the flesh leaving a puncture wound so wide saliva and blood exploded across her face.

Tania leapt to her feet, ever the hard military approach to everything she did, she raised her chin, the blood and saliva mix was already running down her neck. The second coaster launched and she ducked to allow it smash against the wall, leaving a hole in the plasterboard. It bounced along the floor as Dani leapt in the air and dropped a gloved fist into the back of Tania's head, dropping her to the floor.

Dani was completely in slow motion, every punch, every kick perfectly placed. Each blow targeted a different place, until Dani was left with her boot above a barely conscious Tania, her left eye was closed already from the swelling, her right forearm was bent and 45 degrees and her kidneys burned from repeated kicks to her lower back.

Dani stood motionless watching the now weakened Tania. Her right eye flickering in and out consciousness. Dani was cold and calculated at this moment.

A calmness had descended into a darkened view. Dani was now in slow-motion, a silence had fell around her as the pain and rage climbed up her back and whispered in her ear. 'Kill that bitch Tania'.

Dani knelt down beside Tania and shook her head violently, banging it against the floor. The lifeless body of Tania angered Dani, she wanted a spectacular fight to remember, but this lifeless lightweight had barely fought back. She slapped her limp face hard, leaving a red mark with clear finger lines on her cheek. Tania lurched violently to her knees and stared eye to eye with Dani. The look lingered far longer that it should, fire and ice trying to destroy each other. Until Tania leapt forward with both hands and clawed at Dani's hair, the blood red colour of it matching the drying remains of her attack from Dani.

Dani was not fazed by the clawing, she flicked her elbow upwards and caught Tania under the chin sending her flying backwards. Dani's speed was as electrically fast and as agile as a cat. The violence was more like a demonic creature from a horror film. Blow after blow creating an onslaught of pain, specifically placed to bring Tania down again. Each shot hit a particular week point, the elbow to the chin had been followed with a boot stamping on her knee cap, followed by a punch in the ear, with another boot in the kidneys. Violence rained from her as she dropped her knees into the sternum of Tania. The noise was like a dying cow as the oxygen was forced from her chest and her ribs splintered, piercing her left lung and creating even more excruciating pain.

Dani stood over her victim, heavily panting, breathing hard and smiling. She felt good as her prey lay with one eye wide open and tears rolling from it. The closed eye started to shed its pain too. A bloody watery tear trickled along her cheek.

Dani crouched down and whispered in Tania's ear with no fucks, in a growl of a tone tearing at her avenged soul. She whispered *'What would Dan do?'* For the first time in her life fear ran down Tania's spine and she coughed blood into Dani's face.

Dani did not even flinch as the droplets of blood ran down her skin, they dripped from her chin and splashed on to the floor.

"I am both my mother and my father, so ask you self what would they do to you?"

The fear attacked Tania, never had she dealt with this feeling before. The fear of what Dan had done to Dotty's killer raged in Tania's mind, she had read the report many years ago, the terror of what Dan had done with his bike to avenge his family, caused her to cry in fear.

"I ask you again what would Dan do?"

Tania's revelations of her wrong doings flooded her mind, who was she? Is this the end?

The onslaught of emotion had caused her jeans to turn darker between her legs, the smell of piss wafted around Dani's nose. She turned to see the patch grow and the floor become wet. The laugh she gave was purposeful and belittling. She had waited her entire life to humiliate the one who took away both of her parents and here she was enjoying the moment and avenging her parents death. Dani growled again.

"I give so little fucks about you, I don't fear you at all, you are pathetic lying here crying in your own piss and blood...you are nothing!"

The knife she held above Tania was a full tang military style knife with a metal capped end to the handle and engraved letters on it, she plummeted the metal cap straight down into Tania's teeth, terrorising her with agony further. Covered in more blood Tania rolled around in distress with her red and white front teeth now lay on the floor. The cry from her was now deafening and Dani smiled more. Every tear lifted Dani until she felt 10 feet tall.

She reached for her duffel bag on the floor and took out a round pole made of wood, it was aged and dark, not very long but heavy, all the bark had been stripped from it. She placed her foot on the writhing bitch and started to shape the end of the pole into a point, demanding she lay still and watch as the shavings of wood flicked off her pole and landed on Tania.

The fresh bright wood contrasted against the old smooth piece of a tree. This was part of the off cuts her dad had practiced his wood carving skills on. Carefully she placed the large knife back in her jacket and removed a small red pocket knife from her belt. The red scales on the knife were old and scuffed, she tapered the already pointed part to be even sharper at its end, the small knife was sharpened to perfection and sliced through the old part of a tree she had carried for years waiting for this moment.

"Tania, you see this knife? Morris gave this to my dad when he was only 14. He should have given to me as a teenager, but he wasn't there. Jack had to give it me and tell me the stories of this knife and the symbolic moment this was for my dad. How much he used it and the fact that this knife was in his pocket when you shot him"

She skilfully carved her mum and dads initials onto the shaft of the pole and looked at it lovingly, before staring directly at Tania's bloody and swollen face. Never had Tania looked so week. She started to beg for her life. Plead for her to not kill her. The voice was heard and nothing was returned but a stare. The cold icy 1000 yard stare of hurt and pain silently screamed at her.

The moment rested and Tania continued to beg for her life and apologies followed with phrases of *'I was doing my job'* and *'I had to bring him to justice'*.

None of the words effected Dani. None of the false sentiments broke past her reality. None of the pain she saw below her matched the pain she carried daily with her. Agony was oozing from every pore and she was stood with no noise around her, the wild screaming of Tania was muted, she watched as Tania begged in tears but no sound broke through the pain Dani was drowning in. Dani's boot stamped on the already broken ribs below her and blood splattered upwards on to her leg from the now semi-conscious Tania.

A sharp intake of breath lifted Dani's chin high, before she dropped all of her weight holding the stake in her hand. She drove it deep into the chest of the bitch she had dreamed of killing most of her life. The scream Tania let out reverberated around the room and Dani heard it at full volume. She held the death weapon tight and pushed harder until it would go no deeper. Their faces almost touching as Tania let out her last breath with her non swollen eye wide open and then the moment came. Tania went limp beneath her. Dani was motionless and cold. Her eyes emotionless and holding her own breath, listening in delight that Tania had finally been extinguished by her own hand carved stake, she was proud of her avengement.

Pursed lips and now holding her full tang knife, she ran her fingers across the engraving, looking at the letters DAN. She knelt in the blood and piss of Tania. The knife easily carving into the skin on Tania's forehead. She engraved the letters DAN.

A slow and savoured moment. Time appeared to stand still, minutes or hours could have passed, she had no idea. This moment was stored deep in her mind and had left her with a feeling of satisfaction, a glee of pride. A closeness to her father.

A silent exit as the electric bike exited and led her on her escape, no head turns from the people she passed, mundane lives strolled around and did not notice her. The bike effortless and silent, not raising any alarm to what she had done.

She returned to the address she had been given by Joe and had been told to ask for greaser. The gates opened with a clunk and stood in the yard was a tubby man in dirty orange overalls wiping his hands.

"Dani, your bike is over there, Joe told me you were coming. The bunker is prepped as Joe had requested. I ask no questions and I expect no stories, if you need anything I will be in the workshop"

With his gravel voice rattling around her, he marched off, with his battered rigger boots kicking up dust as he walked.

Dani entered the bunker, it was no hotel room, but bolted to the side was a homemade baby changing table and on it was a bottle of whiskey waiting for her with a cheap old phone. The note next it read. Call me.

The thoughts ran through her head and she was imagining who it might be on the other end. She knew of this place. She had heard the story of Greaser and her stay here decades ago. Although she knew the story well she had no recollection of it as she had been a new born on her last stay here.

The mixed emotions of being where her mum and dad had hidden from Tania, just after she had now killed Tania for them, hit her hard and she slumped into the chair swigging from her teat of escapism, numbing her pain.

The hours rolled by and the bottle started to empty. Dani had often found herself, confused, pained and blotting out the pain with drink, drugs and reckless risky behaviour, not to mention the addiction to sex she had. A true wild child who never really had a chance of happiness, with the grief she carried.

Slurred and with no one to hear but herself, the words bumbled out of her mouth.

"I am a normal reaction to a fucked up situation. I am who I am because of what happened. I *am who I am in spite of what happened. I am unique because of what happened and I am fuckin proud of it!"*

The morning sun did not wave in her direction, the bunker was closed off from the outside world, a perfect escape in the middle of everything. It's a place like Harz to her, to sing her sad sad song of pain in.

Dani felt as if her slate was clean, she had erased herself and her grief. Now it was time to start again. Her mumbled voice floated around as she spoke in her sleep.

"Start life again, my pain will wane. Start again you have avenged the Revelator".

The phone rang and shocked her from her slumber. The startled state she was in causing her to tremble. The words on the screen read simply. Answer me!

CHAPTER 12: FOLLOW YOUR HEART

The phone vibrated hard on the wooden surface, bouncing slightly on the solid textured surface, the screen flashed and the fear of answering every prevalent. Dani pressed the answer button and said no words. The gruff voice on the other end was easily recognisable, still she did not want to speak. Feeling the pain in her head from the whiskey and the confused elation yet sorrow of completing her list.

"I know you can hear me Dani, the whole police force is going to be after you. I need you back in Harz ASAP"

Dani welled up and as she opened her mouth to speak, her voice refused to sound. Almost a croak managed to escape, but as much as she tried nothing came. As much as she wanted to tell Jack everything she had done, he clearly already knew. Jack explained his one way conversation. Telling her he would collect her from the place this all started, the words floated around her fluctuating mind as he told her there was a way to collect her and her bike, he had arranged a flight but we are laying low in a hanger. The final words snapped her back into a familiar place with Jack. His authoritative voice forever creating the strength of a father figure.

"Two days from now we leave from Ritchie's. Be Ready. Are we clear?"

A faint voice returned a simple yes as she cancelled the call, she knew the drill, she had spent enough time around Jack and his world, she did as always required, she dropped the phone on the floor and stamped the heel of her boot straight through the phone. She needed to remain incognito. Jack was right this was a moment to remain undercover, a moment to fly under the radar. A moment to remain off grid.

Jack laid back in an old wingback arm chair, a deep oxblood chesterfield that was well worn and suited his feelings now, puffing on his cigar drinking his morning coffee he typed one final message before he smashed the phone against the wall, the words simply said. *'My love, mission complete. Back in two days, when this initial heat has died down around Tania, love Jack xx'*

As Jack relaxed again smoking on his Cuban cigar, the rich smoke floated around him and he drifted in to a day dream of love. The kind of love a man cannot explain, the kind of love reserved for the one, the kind of love that changes a man forever.

Jack had never been a stranger to Harz, he had visited regularly, until Indy's heart softened and they had fell in love. He had followed his love, his heart had lead him back to Indy time after time. He had loved her before she was ready to love anyone, even herself. He would have followed her to the end of the world. He had never loved another woman, but the day he met Indy his world changed. She was the perfect happy hippy and the perfect care free person.

As the years aged her. She mellowed over the grief she carried in her head. The mix of her bullying husband in a forced marriage and what she did to save Dan in that petrol station had took its toll on her. Time was a great healer and she relaxed over her past, her eyes opened to her scruffy angel. The bad boy that cared. Her soul mate.

The relationship they built was strong and every day as the 20 years rolled by he told her multiple times a day how beautiful she was. The banter they exchanged kept them close. Whenever Jack said she was now more beautiful than when he first met her. She always replied with *'But I now have much more weight around my hips and backside than 20 years ago too'*. Jack always smiled and told her *'I know that's my favourite part of you too. You have grown too'* as he tried to show off the psychology he thought he knew about. *'Is that a fat joke?'* she would giggle to him. Ever playful Jack would tell her *'don't be a dick Indy'* she loved it when he was playful like this with her.

Jack was the one who had always followed his dreams and Indy was a dreamer. The match of them had been beautiful. They often joked how they wish they had managed to be together sooner. The reality was, when they were both ready to fall in love, the universe had brought them together to make the perfect loving relationship.

The reality of the present day was not so nice, Jack was back in his old world and Indy was at home worrying about both Jack and Dani. She never wanted either of them to leave the safety of Harz, she was very happy to remain in the perfect hidden off grid palace they had created.

Dani Rode into Ritchie's garage, the huge roller shutter door was wide open she was pleased to be back on her own bike, the bike she was at one with, the bike she felt part of, the bike she adored. Ritchie looked up immediately recognising the bike. A large smile flooded across him and he dropped his tools to close the door behind her.

"Fuck me Dani have you seen the news? You are a fukin' legend. Your name will go down in folk law. Your dad would be proud of you!"

She heard every word and a smile crept across her. It was the first time she had felt those words properly. The first time she had the warmth of her father's memory hug her. Ritchie could see her smile from the side as she pulled of her helmet, but she never turned to allow him to see it fully. She was proud of what she had achieved, however she had still righted a wrong with a wrong. She could not decide if it was better to rule with good or with evil. She knew the mind is the power, she knew we can be surrounded by beauty and see evil and surrounded by evil and see beauty, we make our selves the hero or the martyr, rarely do we see the reality. It's a journey of self-discovery to try and break this cycle.

Dani's heart felt full, she felt happy. She felt complete. Dani looked up at the TV as it flickered into life. Ritchie showed her news reel after news reel. With his phone casting to the TV. Stories of the Avenging biker. The back story of a troubled youth who just wanted to be loved. The reporter she had been so curt with, clearly had her back and had shown both Dan and Dani as lost souls trying to do the right thing. A disturbed hero and heroine that had fought fire with fire. The old age debate of right and wrong raged on the social media platforms. With most people appearing to side with the lost girl who needed her father.

Social media had dubbed her the Avenging Angel, however the police were searching for her and calling her a vicious murderer, a danger to society, CCTV footage of her on the silent electric bike now circulating around the internet. Comments underneath flooding support for her. As Ritchie flicked though the comments she slumped to the floor leaning against her bike. Wishing that instead of her fifteen minutes of fame. She actually had her father with her. To have known him as her legend. Not the legend that everyone else saw. As much as she loved the fact he had always be adored by many, she never had that special insight to him. The insight only a daughter could have and with that she stood tall and smiled.

"Fuck that bitch Tania and everyone that had crossed my dad"

A huge roar of a bike made her jump as her words left her mouth, startling her from her moment. Ritchie had started the bike that was her Dad's, the triple twisted monster of a cruiser. The one that her dad met her mother on. The bike that she had felt she was not ready to ride.

"So are you ready now?"

Ritchie's words were still bouncing around when she jumped on the bike. It felt like home it felt like she belonged now. The roller shutter door started to click and clang its way to its open position. The look on her face was enough for Ritchie to know. To know she was ready to feel this bike, feel closer to her father and finally put the past to rest.

The rear of the bike disappeared into the countryside and Ritchie stood proud. It had taken him years to get that bike from the police and longer to restore it, the drop into the estuary had ruined all of the electrics and most of the mechanicals were rusted. The effort for him was rewarded as he saw the bike disappear and a lone biker stood outside dressed in black with a black helmet and a black visor, who saluted him before vanishing in front of him. Ritchie's smile warmed his entire soul.

The old bruiser of a cruiser had long been forgotten about and as she slipped out into the countryside, she had a few places to see before Jack would pick her up.

The abyss of society rolled along around her, she had no desire to be part of this world. Things that Indy had fondly spoke of attracted her though, places her dad had enjoyed visiting. Places she wanted to feel close to him in.

Standing in the National Memorial Arboretum. She visited the wall. The wall had thousands of names on it, thousands of names who had been killed serving honour and thousands of families who would have mourned their loved ones who had passed. She felt an odd sentimental feeling. Her dads name was not on this wall and nor should it be, but many fathers names were on this wall. Suddenly she felt an affinity with these people a solidarity. We all have suffering. Her suffering was the same yet different. The real world was beckoning yet she still did not want it. As she rounded the memorial the haunting empty walls struck her. Space had been left for thousands of names to join the memorial of already fallen heroes.

All Dani wanted was her own paradise, hurting no one, providing for her own and others alike. She knew happiness is not given by others, nor possessions, it's a far simpler pleasure, feeling the sun rise and fall in the same day, achieving good for ourselves and the chosen few we share our deepest love with. By being temperate and disciplined in this progress and stepping forward each day. She desperately wanted to achieve an altruistic hippy life. Rejoicing in the small happiness she would build striving to just be better than she was yesterday. Creating the perfect internal world, this is why Dan had always asked how is your world? Not how are you? It was a phrase Indy now said daily and Dani loved to hear it.

Indy had told her many things about her father, things that now seemed clearer to her, as if before she was not ready to listen.

Dan was a sigma male, but he had needed the one who could bring him peace. He found the one in Joanne, but there time was cut short. Indy tried to teach her not to wait too long to accept we all need the one, even if you think you don't. You do!

Dani revelated on her life, could she be happy ? Would Otto still love her like he clearly always had. Could she have a second chance after rebuffing him so many times? Could her and Otto create what Jack and Indy had? Indy had rejected Jack Many times before and they still fell in love years later.

Dani's revelations of life were changing here. Stood in the middle of the wall of names thousands of people killed in war. She had a chance, but was it too late to follow her heart? Had she sabotaged her own life? How can she shed her pain for good? How can she create her paradise?

CHAPTER 13: EPIPHANY

A short slow ride on her dads bike led her along some tight twisting roads. A huge hill in front of her, it was time to head homeward and get some rest before Jack arrived, the huge bike was a brute for her to control, especially around small country roads, a pretty old church loomed into view. It was heavily overgrown and had a small graveyard to the side of it. A moment of piece was ahead, a moment of reflection and a moment to rest. The emotions were running high and Dani was very home sick.

Gingerly she skulked into the church and sat down near the back unseen by anyone. The old wooden seat was cold and hard, the air was damp. Gold and red velvet was draped over the alter. Dani had no desire to ask for forgiveness or ask for guidance. She wanted a sanctuary and to be left alone.

An eerie coldness was lurking in the air, the building was quiet and still. The absence of sound was a comforting feeling for Dani. A door at the rear of the church opened and a man dressed in a black robe with his white band showing around his neck appeared. He hadn't noticed her as he started to tidy around the altar. His mannerisms were slow but meaningful as he shuffled around at the back of the church. Dani watched with idle curiosity, until he looked across at her and smiled, the type of smile only an old man can give.

He nodded and started to walk in her direction, his voice was croaky as he spoke to her. He asked her questions that she found odd. He asked if she wanted a black coffee, if the road had taught her well and if the Rocket was looking after her.

Dani was confused and her faced showed it, her expression questioning how this man would ask such precise questions and know so much before she spoke.

"Are you the daughter of Dan?"

Her face now changed to that of shock, a face of confused shock. This old vicar knew of her dad and realised who she was. She could not work out how at all?

He continued with his wobbly old voice to tell her that the black behemoth outside is Dan's bike, it has parked out the front of this church many times. It's been many years since I last saw it though.

Dani was reeling in confusion at the tale she was being told. The vicar stood in front of her and said.

"Please come and have a coffee with me, your dad always did. It's far too early for whiskey anyway"

It was clear this man knew her father, was this a trap? Was her first thought, was this how she got caught? Lured in by a friendly old man, Dani was not fearful of anyone at all and nodded as she followed the old preacher to a back room. The little office had an old ornate desk and a modern coffee machine on it, with a pack of biscuits sat next to it.

"That bike only parked there when Dan was questioning himself of life and now it's here again but with you, what brings you to me?"

Dani hung her head low and explained, she had been told of this place by Indy and she said Dan loved it here. The vicar nodded and agreed with her. She explained how she had never known her father and she was on a journey learning all about him. The vicar nodded as he explained, every person had always spoken highly of her Dad. She felt closer to her dad than ever right now, she could almost feel his presence.

The man of the cloth spoke fondly of a respectful man who questioned everything about life. Things like: are we in a computer simulation? Are we actually from this planet? Was god actually an alien?

"He certainly questioned me hard on religion and the good book"

The old man explained how the last time he saw Dan, he told him of Plato and the Stoics. He explained how excited Dan was and keen to learn new things, especially on how to live one's life well. I hoped I would see him again someday, however I saw the news years ago and the result of the police encounter with him and I believe the woman who killed him, is being buried here this afternoon.

"Is that why you are here?"

Dani recoiled and furrowed her brow with a pensive stare, not sure how this man would have guessed her plan. She stood and paced back and forth not really saying anything, until she gathered herself together and took a large deep breath. She asked the question that had been bothering her, the question that was paining her, the question that could hurt her mentally now. But she asked it anyway.

"If you kill, are you evil? Can a wrong right a wrong? What if there was a good reason?"

He explained how nothing is ever right or wrong, who can dictate other than God? It's just our perception of it. Things that were deemed okay decades and centuries before are no longer seen as okay. Does that make them wrong or just your interpretation? We once thought it was okay to send children in to the mines or up chimneys. Now this would seem barbaric. Dani's face was twisted with confusion. Her eyes looking upwards as she tried to work out her thoughts, not sure if she believed any longer that she had done right or if her father had done right also.

The cleric watched her body language and sat silently still whilst she tried to make sense of what that meant to her.

"Dani I had this same chat with your father, what has been done cannot be changed, if you break the modern laws, you are guilty. However did you break them for the right reasons? All war is murder, it's just been agreed that's okay. Was it for good or evil. That is the question to answer"

With that thought dancing in her mind. Dani was secure once again and knew she had broken the law. This however was her war, a war like a Viking, in her world she can only answer to Odin. The light shone through the open doorway and illuminated her red dreadlocked hair with short cropped sides. She felt like a Viking too. War had taken place, honour had been restored and her family had been avenged. She had set the record straight.

Gracefully and kindly she kissed him on the forehead and thanked him for his kind words. Her mind was straightening out. She was justifying her actions and those of her father. The behemoth bike vociferously and violently left the car park with dust and dirt thrown up behind her and she was gone.

The Pastor smiled and shook his head, '*Two peas in a pod, Dani and her father are*', he thought to himself.

The church started to fill up with uniformed officers and high ranking officials. The air was sombre and the mood flat. A small service explained her devotion to the police service and her marriage to the job. No one shed a tear, lots of respect was felt but many had also felt the wrath of Tania too, she was not the most well liked person in the force and no family members attended at all. Nobody knew if she even had family. She certainly had never mentioned them.

The coffin was carried out by four very large police officers in full uniform, the silence was deafening as the officers carried the coffin with no music played and a deathly quiet in the air. The coffin had been laid on the ground ready to be lowered into its final resting place, on it was a drape with the force's crest upon it, with her police uniformed hat and black leather gloves on the top of the coffin, the pall bearer officers, stood back wearing their white gloves still very bright white and fresh.

A small prayer was slowly wafting along the crisp cool air from the clergyman. The officers had already noticed a woman stood in the distance all in black with bright red hair. Two officers whispered to each other, '*maybe it's a long lost daughter?*' stifled laughter nearly escaped to ruin the moment.

Thunderous noise overshadowed the whispering officers as the huge black bike bellowed as it rode straight at them, red dreadlocked hair flowing out the back of the black helmet contrasting with the all black look. The huge bike skidded sideways with the rear wheel locked up throwing mud in the air as it slid towards the coffin, the noise of splintering wood exploded as the bike clattered into the casket.

The wooden box left the ground and crashed against the side of the grave. Splitting the coffin wide open and leaving Tania's body exposed for all to see as it ricocheted its way to the bottom of the grave with her body hanging half out of the coffin.

The silence was well and truly gone. Horror and gasps around the cemetery as the bike exited in a cloud of smoke and dust. The mourners all open mouthed and starting to gather around the now open box, to catch a glimpse of the atrocity.

Dani had not wanted a peaceful burial for Tania. She had wanted to embarrass her for one last time and this was it. Helpless, lifeless and laid bare for all to see.

By the time the officers had all taken a look at Tania. Dani was long gone, even the loud exhaust had faded into the distance as she ran for the sun, hoping never to be seen again.

Dani had her epiphany, Dani had her mind in order and she knew she had lived with her anger so long, she was on first name terms with it. The feelings of hate were melting away, the feeling of anger subsiding and the feeling of avengement now turning into pride. She was who she was in spite of everything not because of it. This was it. This was her time to start again.

The journey south had blurred into a nothing. It was not even a memory. She had not focused on anything but her new world. How would she re start? What would she want life to look like? Who would be in that life? The revelations of wanting happiness but shedding the pain was still going to take time. The ghosts of torture do not leave easily.

The black beast was sat on its side stand, the ticking noises raised themselves up in the air, from the metal as it cooled down showing how hot the bike had got on this fast blast south, escaping the mess she had created. All of the mud from the funeral assault was still plastered around the bike too.

As she sat at the back of Ritchie's garage, she felt contentment like she had never felt before. She no longer felt like Tania was laughing at her family and along the way she had rectified some bad feelings too, she had improved the world. In her mind she was right, having restored some balance into society, educating the horrors of society. The sun was just starting to drop in the sky and the light was dimming, the air was cooling and a small rustling sound behind Dani made her jump.

Stood now ready to fight she saw a Staffordshire Bull Terrier with oil soaked fur, shivering, with his tail between his legs. A strong powerful dog looking weak and downtrodden. The sight of a dog always excited her. This one was scared and thin, with ribs protruding and with rubbish stuck to the drenched oily fur and no collar.

As she approached it, the dog growled, its eyes were not aggressive but his growl telling her he was scared. The closer she looked she saw scars protruding from the wet coat and many fresh scratch marks. Ignoring the growls she reached down to him and he whimpered, tucked himself into the corner next to the bins and tried to hide from her in the shadows.

This oil covered dog was a tortured soul who had been abused, possibly as he would not fight, due to his nice nature. His cuts and scratches looked like those of a fighting dog. She persevered until he let her fuss him behind his ear. He let out the biggest Staffordshire Bull Terrier smile before jumping all over her. The next few hours were spent cleaning the oil from him. The oil was golden and difficult to remove from his coat. Trying to clean him up as best she could and feed him was a funny experience, as the more she tried the more he tried to cuddle into her. This was possibly the first time he had seen kindness in his short life.

"Slick, I shall call you slick as you were covered in oil"

Just as Ritchie came out to bring her more supplies, the unmistakable sound of a Chinook, the twin rotor noise getting louder and louder. Ritchie nodded as the 200MPH monster loomed over the building.

CHAPTER 14: NEW BEGININGS

Dirt and grit flung in the air, the noise deafening as the monstrous helicopter's twin propellers and twin engine noise assaulted everyone's ears. The slap and snap noise of the two whirling rotors taking over the entire area. The side door was open and a long bearded old man was half leaning out of the gap with a huge cigar in between his teeth. Her breath steadied as she smiled. Dani placed her steampunk googles over her eyes and her neck warmer over her mouth. She knew this was her escape. Jack was here and that meant safety. Jack had been the closest thing to a father she ever had. Whenever she had needed saving he always appeared.

The dust hung in the air and the big green troop carrier was still not quite on the ground as Jack stepped off with a semi-automatic machine gun in one hand and his hunting knife in the other. The smile on his face shone passed the cigar still gripped in his aged yellow teeth.

Dani ran up to him and threw her arms around the old veteran. He was in full camo gear, with black and green war paint on his face, with his trousers tucked into his combat boots and a bandanna holding back his long hair. The blades slowed and the noise dropped to a whine. Jack tucked his knife in his belt and took the cigar out of his mouth, smoke seeped out of his crooked smile as he spoke, making him look like a pirate.

"Well you are Dan's daughter and then some."

Her pride bubbled up and she felt warm. She was her father's daughter. She was like him in many ways and Jacks approval was almost as good as hearing it from Dan himself. Jack and Dan were like peas in a pod. Ritchie sauntered out as the blades slowed wearing his aviator sunglasses and talking about the engines in the 'old big bird'.

"Come on you Maverick wannabee, get the bike in and lets go"

He loaded the white triple and Jack immediately leapt in to action strapping it down in the cargo bay, As Ritchie threw a leg over the old black behemoth to load that too. Dani strutted her way over to him and hit the kill switch. She leaned forward and kissed him on the forehead, she explained how much respect she had for him and cannot thank him enough for what he has done for her, her dad and Indy let alone Jack.

"Keep it Ritchie, put it with the Streetfighter my dad built and the one that Morris created, ride them all and keep them next to each other on display, the complete story of Dan. You deserve it my old friend"

Ritchie's eyes bulged and tears filled them, he was in shock, he wanted that trilogy of bikes, but would never have asked for her to leave any of those bikes, he had presumed he was loading them all.

Dani had the bike she wanted, the one built by Ritchie emulating her dad, he built it for her just like Morris had had for Dan.

As she strode to the helicopter her kick ass stride extenuated her legs and her curvy bum. Ritchie was to full of emotion to notice her. He shouted the words.

"You are just like your dad"

Her stride never missed a beat. Her strut confident and her tears now running down her face as Jack helped her into the helicopter, he laid his hand on her shoulder and asked if she was okay. She winked and smiled forcing an even larger tear to roll down her cheek. She cleared her throat and turned back to look out of the door.

"Here boy, come on Slick"

The Staffy, bounded towards them with the huge smile only a Staffy can give. Jumping into the helicopter and skidding into Jack's legs. With a shake of his head he chuckled to himself and motioned a circular motion with his finger for his comrade to start the engines.

As the Chinook rotors made the familiar twin rotor noise the excitement built in them all, even Slick sat with his mouth wide open and his huge grin beaming with his tongue hanging out of the side. Ritchie sat on the old black beast as the old big bird left the ground, the noise thumping into him and the swirls of dirt surrounding him.

The helicopter stayed low as it crossed the fields. A screech of tyres ricocheted off the buildings and flashing blue lights came in to view. Dani grabbed the machine gun from Jack and shot wildly at the police cars.

"Fuck you fuck you all. This is my time now"

Her words unheard over the pandemonium scene. Bullets fired, tyres screeched and the twin engines blades thumped along.

The helicopter started to raise up from the fields and Dani snatched the belt of grenades hanging at the side of the door. The bombs were launched out of the open cargo door and explosion after explosion rose up from the ground in front of the police cars. Orange and red flames leapt from the ground and engulfed the cars that could not avoid the grenades.

Jack pulled her back by her jacket, knocking her to the floor.

"What would Dan do? He would stop. He had morals!"

The juxta position of being told she was like her dad and now suggesting his morals were higher than hers tormented her. Slick looked at her crest fallen and forlorn with his mouth now closed, as she drew her feet in towards her and sat crying, Slick snuggled into her neck and licked her tears from her face. She slept cuddled up to her dog for most of the flight across Europe, whispering to her new best friend over and over again.

"This is our new beginning"

The pilot was under strict instructions to drop on the coordinates, unload and be gone before they are traced. The precision landing in the Harz mountains was an easy one for such an accomplished veteran. Indy was already running from the garden with her long flowing hippy dress flapping behind her, as soon as the noise from the massive choppers had approached her, she knew it was Dani and Jack.

As they stood on Harz soil once more it felt like home. The taxi they had used disappeared into the sky and Indy ran down the dirt road to them, a familiar two stroke noise pinged its way up the hill from the distance. Indy showered Dani and Jack with kisses. Indy's smile and tears all rolled into one and she cried her happiness aloud at having them both back safe. Slick jumped up at her and she dropped to her knees fussing him and showering him with kisses too. He was just happy to be loved and not tortured anymore, being adored and hugged made his happy meter reach full.

The Two stoke noise exploded over the hill as a flash of orange and black leapt into the air, rear brake already on before the landing and a huge skid until he reached them. He grabbed Dani harder than she had ever been grabbed before, pulled her in tight and hugged her harder than she had ever been hugged before. She felt a strength from him she had never seen. It was the first time she had ever looked at him like a man. It was the first time he had shown her his dominance. It was the first time she had ever truly fancied him. She needed an alfa male, not a boy.

Hans and Sofia trotted up to join the embrace. This was the welcome home feeling everyone needed, to feel loved. The sun started to set and Jack started to tell the story of a kick ass Dani creating mayhem. He never mentioned anything other than just how amazing she was.

The evening had been long and lots of stories told. Dani had been amazed at the synthetic petrol Otto had developed that causes no damage to old vehicles or new, it worked in both petrol and diesel engines. He had been perfecting it on the local farm vehicles without telling anyone and now was ready to produce gallons of it at once in the barn.

Dani told Indy she loved her, that she was a perfect parent, but had not been ready to accept her love as she grew up. She had carried to much pain in her heart, her mind and her very being, to be able to take on any other emotion at all and one day wants to be more like her.

Now the pain is easing she can become like her as well as her mum and dad.

"I am a normal reaction to a fucked up situation"

Indy nodded in agreement and told Dani, that she had a pure heart and never wanted to stop her destiny, never wanted to change who she was.

"You are all of us."

Dani cried and wanted to be more Joanne and Indy, with the strength of her dad. Dani fell asleep on the sofa with a half drunk bottle of whiskey and Slick resting his chin on her thigh. She felt more content now than she had ever felt in her entire life, she felt at home.

The weeks had flicked passed and Dani's return with Slick had been joyous, she took regular rides out in the side car outfit, with Slick in the chair. Even Otto had taken to riding with Slick, sitting by his side in the two seater attached to the bike. Everywhere they went the dog was adored, his huge Staffy grin dominated his face as he sat with his front paws up on the hand rail of the chair. Danni rode with care for her beloved dog and the man she had always nearly loved for years. She now knew her feelings had not been ready to love anyone, including herself.

Slick had changed her, he loved her unconditionally and she learned to let her emotions flood through her. The more she saw the response of people wanting to fuss the dog the more she realised how special he was. Each daft smile, each tail wag, each huge lick from his tongue had melted her. She felt the love from her new companion; she relaxed and wanted to be loved. Now she was in love with Otto and desperate to tell him.

As they all pulled up in front of a lake she had visited many times in her past when she was carrying many heavy black clouds in her mind. A place she had used to help her focus. A place she had used to revelate. She squeezed into the side car with Otto and Slick. The sun was setting and a deep red glow was forming. She placed her hand on Slick's head and said the three words he had allowed her to learn. Her gaze fell upon Otto and she placed a hand on his thigh, his head turned slowly towards her, creating a silhouette in the sunset around his masculine face. The moment blossomed and her heart felt like it grew two sizes that very second as the words escaped from her lips.

"I love you Otto"

His heart felt as if it was bouncing around inside his chest.

"It's about time Dani, I love you too"

The sun hung lower and Slick curled up on their lap, a meeting of lips for the first time. An electrostatic connection, as if they were lost souls who had met many times in different lifetimes and had now found each other again in this one. It was a kiss that intensified their love and magnified their feelings. Slick felt the love in the chair too. He felt so happy with his new family and fell asleep as they cuddled into the sidecar seats.

The morning sun rose the next day, Dani and Otto packed the bike outfit with food and water. The music played in the garage café and the smell of coffee hung in the air as Dani filled up the flasks. Slick wandered around sniffing all the bikes before jumping into the side car and curling up in the chair. Hans and Sofia wandered into the paradise of their world with love and happiness floating around them. They carried two urn's. Dani frowned and stopped dead in her tracks, the music appeared to fade away and she saw the beautiful vessels that had held her parents for decades. Otto gently laid his hand on her hip from behind and drew her close to him; she tensed and went to pull away. He whispered.

"Set them free, let them ride once more"

Her lips tensed and her buttocks clenched in her retro dungarees, the black leather jacket skimmed her waist and the red rockabilly head scarf with cherries on it finished her look.

Sofia smiled, she admired the outfit Dani was wearing. She knew the headscarf and dungarees were Dotty's and the jacket was Joanne's, the side car outfit her dad and Morris had built, this was defiantly a family affair.

Dani climbed into the chair with Slick, he nuzzled into her soft leather jacket, he really had tamed her, by showing her what unconditional love felt like. He had changed her outlook on life and although her natural reaction was often tense with a desire to ride solo. She now yearned for her family to be around her. The sound of old school v twins potatoed their way in as Jack and Indy pulled up outside. Tears of happiness rolled down Indy's cheeks as she saw Dani's beaming smile and her retro outfit she was dressed in.

Dani had picked a spot near a lake that her Dad had written about in his notebooks and where she had always felt calmed. This was where she would scatter the ashes and be able to come and sit to revelate her life, feeling closer to her mum and dad with each passing moment. The small group all nodded and the sidecar outfit led the way with Otto proudly riding the old machine. The bikes rumbled away and an old couple shuffled over to an old café racer next to the coffee machine, the old lady wearing a red polka dot headband with red ruby lipstick on her lips, she smirked as she looked at her old lover stood before her, dressed in turned up jeans and a heavily worn leather jacket.

Two old spirts reunited, Morris walked over to the jukebox and hit the side of it, instantly Dotty's favourite song burst in to life. She smiled a wry smile and asked him.

"Well there cowboy, do you have one last ride in you?"

He winked and smiled.

"Do you though? It's been a long time since you rode pillion"

She teased him as the bike needed kicking twice, before it burst in to life.

"Losing your touch with these old bikes!"

Morris chuckled and they jumped on the old café racer that used to be attached to the side car and rode off to watch the scattering of the ashes,

"Dan are you coming son?"

A black leather clad biker on a black bike with a black helmet and a black visor accelerated passed on his back wheel; he nodded as he showboated along the dusty rode chasing Danni and her pack.

As he screamed passed the side car outfit, Dani saw the black biker that she had seen following her through her revelations. She now knew who it was, she recognised the bike. It was Dad.

Tears filled her eyes as they rode the side car across the grass to the lake, as the ashes were slowly scattered across the water that glistened with sun kissed glitter. Dani knew it was time to live, create her life before it was too late, rather than chasing ghosts. Slick sat stern and still next to her foot, leaning slightly against her leg. Otto had his arm around her and stood pensive as they mourned the losses once again.

Indy unpacked the picnic she had in the boot of the side car, she started pouring tea and laying out food of all varieties, Slick turned and watched as the smell of deli meats and pastries flicked across his nose, it twitched with delight of what he might be given to him. With them all sat in a circle on the red tartan blanket the mood was sombre yet happy. Dani let out a big smile and took a sharp intake of breath as she watched the 3 people stood on the hillside. A café racer and black custom streetfighter behind the three of them, let her know her dad was proud of her.

Indy looked over her shoulder to see them too. This was the end but the beginning. She winked and told a story she had told Dani many times before. A story of Dan planning to take Joanne to a castle in England. He had bought a ruby ring as Joanne had always adored them. He had planned to ride to the castle, stand at the top of the tower and propose to Joanne.

Dani looked down with a heavy heart. She had searched for the ring that her dad had bought her mum, but had never found it. Otto's smile was huge as he looked at Indy. He had found the ring in the bottom draw of a tool box in small hinged box a few weeks before and showed it Indy. The Smile she returned to Otto was pure happiness. The next planned exploration was Bodiam Castle. Otto had his plan to take Dani to Sussex and stand at the top of the mystical castle with its moat beneath them to propose.

Otto had seen the bikers on the hill too. Indy saw Otto dreaming of the proposal, she knew his plans. He knew the old bikers would be forever watching over them like guardian angels. Dani caught the smiles between them and asked what was going on and they giggled telling her. It's surprise and if you ask questions you will only be told, I can neither confirm nor deny.

She pulled Slick in close to her and cuddled him, the feeling of loss weighed heavy on her, but the feeling of excitement equally lifted her. Slick had opened her heart. She now felt love and wanted to give love. Dani stood up and her red dreadlocked hair flicked over her shoulder as she turned.

"Come on then you lot, these bikes wont ride themselves"

The bikers rode up in to the Harz mountains with the sun on their backs and a stunning sunset hanging in the air. Buried deep in her mind was the gleeful memories of avenging her parents deaths, the split blood still making her smile and the new feeling of being able to love illuminating her soul. Life felt balanced as she had exorcized her demons and knew in her heart, old bikers never die, they just ride in your shadow to protect you.

Her demons now rested easy and her life could begin. It was now time to restart her life, re-invent herself and become the person she always should have been. Time to be the star in her own life.

The End

Mark Huck was born in 1970's, growing up in the fast paced 1980's living an adrenaline filled life, with sports and fast cars; as his life became more complex he found his solidarity in the simplicity of the open road and the world of motorbikes.

After leaving school with barely any qualifications his love of engines led him to become a mechanic, a love that would never leave him, drawing him more and more to the world he now lives in; as he moved into the world of teaching mechanical studies, he put right the poor education by completing as many qualifications as he could.

As children came along, responsibility beckoned, life was happy and quaint, but the desire for adrenaline always bubbled. Now with the children having jobs and lives of their own, Mark is now living a fast paced adrenaline filled life with a desire to escape the "norms" of society.

Avenged Revelator is Mark's final book of a trilogy, a story inspired by real life stories and events that have only happened in the depth of imagination.

Printed in Great Britain
by Amazon